# CHAMELEON

## RICHARD PAULLIN

*Cover Art Cayte Butler*

ISBN: 978-1-961879-02-7 (sc)
978-1-961879-03-4 (e)

Publishing rev. date:  08/06/2023

# CHAMELEON

# CHAPTER 1

Unbeknownst to her parents or anyone else, ten-year-old Nadine had already decided her life's career, unusual for a child at such an early age, but Nadine was no ordinary child. She knew she was smarter than her classmates and her teachers, but she didn't want anyone to know: not her classmates, not her teachers, not even her parents. She purposely underperformed in her schoolwork. Her lackluster academic performance didn't concern her teachers. They were far more concerned with her social behavior since she showed no interest in making friends.

This set off alarm bells at the Percival Peabody Preparatory School where Nadine was a fourth-grade student. One morning Peabody's twenty-six-year-old social worker, Ms. Madelaine Eckhart-Cochran, rode the elevator to the seventh floor of the William Walker Apartment Complex and pushed the buzzer to the Car residence. Nadine's mother opened the door.  Ms. Cochran introduced herself, placing special emphasis on the fact she was a social worker representing Triple P, an acronym she frequently used because she felt it gave her added importance and the moral authority to say whatever she wished and to snoop wherever she pleased.  Mrs. Car motioned for her to enter the apartment.

Ms. Cochran wasted no time in getting to the point of her visit. "I want you to realize, Mrs. Car," she said in a snooty voice, "it is my obligation to the Triple P community to make certain all the needs of every student are met at school and in the home to ensure all Triple P students are headed in the proper direction. Show me Nadine's room."

Mrs. Car led her to Nadine's room. Ms. Cochran was struck by the room's plainness with its white window curtains and a plain white bedspread covering the neatly made bed. The room's sparseness prompted her to ask, "Why are there no stuffed animals and other things a ten-year-old girl should have?" Before Mrs. Car could answer, Ms. Cochran added, "At least you allow Nadine to have a computer."

Ms. Cochran abruptly turned toward the closet. She opened its doors and surveyed the few clothes that hung neatly on hangers. She removed a purple dress from the closet and held it up for Mrs. Car to see. "Why don't you buy her appropriate clothes? She is a constant embarrassment to the Triple P community when she wears dresses like this."

"Her father and I have offered many times to take her to expensive stores, but she demands we shop only at thrift shops. She says she's doing it to save us money because she knows we're not rich. Maybe we're not rich, but we can certainly afford to buy her better clothes."

Ms. Cochran sniffed an "I see" and left.

Several days later, a Dr. Sidney C. Grimes called Mrs. Car. In a superior sounding voice, he introduced himself as a board-certified psychiatrist who represented those students at the Percival Peabody Preparatory School who demonstrated some type of psychiatric disorder. "The reason for my call, Mrs. Car, is that Ms. Eckhart-Cochran at the Peabody School has notified me that Nadine has no friends and is not interested in making any. This is a concern to me as well because it represents an abnormal attitude toward society as a whole. This most alarming situation brings to the forefront concerns about Nadine's psycho-sexual health especially in a prepubescent young girl. Have you noticed any abnormal changes in Nadine's sexual behavior? I ask this, Mrs. Car, to ascertain if Nadine shows any propinquity for the same sex. If so, I can enroll her in groups that offer support to a female child who may be in the early stages of becoming a lesbian or perhaps in the early stages of questioning her present sexual assignment. There are any number of groups who can guide Nadine through these life-altering processes. Has Nadine commented on her sexual assignment?"

"She most certainly has not, nor have I or her father ever considered such a thing." The anger in Mrs. Car's voice startled even her since she hadn't raised her voice to such a level in years. "Besides, such matters are none of your business nor is it the business of anybody at the Peabody School. I can assure you Nadine is a perfectly normal child. She may not be the brightest or the best-dressed student at Peabody, but she does the best she can, and so do her mother and father, and...and...and for your information...her father and I love our daughter very much," whereupon Mrs. Car pressed the end call button on her cell phone.

# CHAPTER 2

The walls of the William Walker Apartment Complex did little more than separate apartment from apartment and room from room allowing Nadine to hear all of what her neighbors and some of what her parents had to say. Her neighbors were easy to hear because they screamed all day long about money and sex. Nadine had a more difficult time hearing her parents' conversations because both were soft-spoken even when they had disagreements, and those few disagreements centered on her and her clothes.

Since Nadine was such a docile child, neither her father nor her mother wished to make an issue of the way she dressed so they decided to let her dress the way she wanted. Nevertheless, they worried what her teachers, her classmates, and their parents might think of Nadine and them for the shabby way she looked. Both realized they were sending to school a child that looked more like a waif than the daughter of a successful accountant.

One evening Nadine overheard her mother tell her father about Ms. Cochran's visit and Dr. Grimes's phone call. She could hear the distress in her mother's voice as she described both incidents. Then she heard her mother's soft, sobbing voice, "Oh, Howard, what are we going to do?" and her father's gentle voice trying to calm her.

Nadine had originally thought if she looked different no one would pay attention to her, but the opposite had happened. Rather than deflect attention, the difference had brought unwanted attention in the form of Cochran and Grimes. She decided she had to change her plan, not too radically, but enough to get those two off her back.

The next trip to the thrift shop she selected two white blouses, two blue sweaters, and two blue skirts. She knew these clothes would please her parents, and she hoped Cochran and Grimes so they would mind their own business and stop bothering her and her parents. As for her classmates, she could care less what they thought.

# CHAPTER 3

Nadine never wanted to betray or lose her parents' trust because that would unnecessarily complicate or completely shut down her plans. To allay any fears her parents might have about her use of the computer, she rearranged the bedroom furniture so she would be in full view. When her mother asked why she had rearranged her room, Nadine answered in a reassuring manner, "I'm going to do some research on the computer, Mommy, and I don't want you to think I'm looking at bad things. My bedroom door will always be open." Her mother smiled and wondered how she could have been so lucky to have such a wonderful child. In the days and weeks that followed, Nadine was pleased her plan worked. Her parents walked past her room with nary a glance knowing that whatever she was doing on the computer was harmless.

Nadine had a photographic memory that enabled her to learn and retain complex material. Because of this ability, she realized she was smart. How smart she didn't know so she issued a personal challenge: to learn to speak, write, and understand French in less than a year. She figured if she could learn French then Italian, Portuguese, and Spanish wouldn't be far behind. She researched the Internet and found numerous free sites where she could learn the language from native-born French speakers. Within three weeks, she could carry on a simple conversation. After three months, she was fluent.

The rest of the year she spent learning Italian, Portuguese, and Spanish. Next, she decided to really test herself with German. German took a little more time as did Russian, Arabic, and Chinese, but she mastered them all.

Then it happened shortly after she turned thirteen. One morning as she stared into the bathroom mirror, she was horrified by what she saw. She had been so intent on learning languages she hadn't noticed what had been happening to her, yet there it was, as plain as the perfect nose on her face along with full lips, high cheekbones, perfectly arched eyebrows, and to accent nature's bounty, deep blue eyes shaded by dark, long lashes. "Oh, no," she uttered to herself. "This can't be happening. Not to me! I don't want to be pretty."

A sudden, frightful thought occurred to her.  She quickly unbuttoned her baggy pajama top to look at her breasts: something she hadn't done for some time because she had no interest in them.  When she looked in the full-length mirror attached to the closed bathroom door, she groaned in agony. Her breasts had more than doubled in size. "*Oh, no,* she thought to herself.  *These are going to be a problem.*  She hoped they wouldn't grow any larger, but that was not to be.

# CHAPTER 4

From past experience, Nadine realized she needed to fit in: to be as unnoticed as possible. When she was fifteen, a new hairstyle, the frizzy look, captured the hearts and minds of young and older women alike who thought the style fun and sexy. Nadine's brownish-blonde hair was the proper length for the new hairstyle. She followed the directions she found on the Internet. With a little teasing, her hair blossomed into a large *frizzy-flower* as she liked to call it. The effect pleased her because the hairstyle detracted from her facial features.

Nevertheless, she was concerned her blue eyes might still give away her attractiveness. She convinced her parents to buy her glasses even though the optometrist assured them she had perfect vision, but to satisfy their daughter's whim, they finally agreed to buy a pair of black frame, non-corrective-lens glasses. There was one other thing Nadine wanted: brown contacts to match her hair so she said, but it was to cover her blue eyes. Nadine smiled when the optometrist placed the brown, non-corrective contacts in her eyes that completely hid the blueness of her own. She issued a second smile when the optometrist placed the black- framed glasses on her face, a smile that melted her parents' heart. Seeing their daughter pleased with the new look, her parents beamed with pride.

Nadine's classmates took little notice of her frizzed hair or the black-framed glasses. They considered her weird. They passed her in the hallways and sat next to her in classes, but seldom did anyone speak to her except to say in a disgusted tone, "Nadine, will you get the hell out of my way." This lack of attention pleased her.

With the physical appearance crisis fixed and foreign language classes finished, she could focus on another aspect of her career plan. She joined a local theatrical group to learn about make-up, wigs, clothes design, their alteration, prosthetics, quick changes, and all the tricks of the backstage theatrical trade. The director of the group was pleased to have someone as young as Nadine take an interest in backstage crafts. She lamented that every young person who approached her only wanted to be a star and famous.

Shortly after Nadine joined the theatrical group, she searched the Internet for sites that specialized in a variety of professions from computer geniuses to locksmith specialists who could help her with several problems that confronted her if her plan was to succeed. One evening, she found the site she had been looking for. She was engrossed in its content when she heard her father's voice. He was standing behind her looking at the monitor. She jumped. "Sorry to scare you, sweetheart. Whatcha doin' so late?"

Nadine had practiced for this situation so she wouldn't be unprepared. After the first fright faded, she looked up at him and said, "I'm in a mess, Daddy. I'm doing research for a book, and my heroine is locked in a room with an electro-magnetic lock on the door. Any suggestions on how to get her out?"

"None. I'm afraid you've painted yourself into a corner."

"I'm afraid you're right. Oh, well, I'll have to think of something else."

"Let me know how you solve your locked door problem," he said over his shoulder as he started toward the door.

"I already have. She'll use a key." Both laughed.

"Night, sweetheart." She could hear his retreating footsteps on the hardwood floor.

Nadine sighed a sigh of relief, went to bed, and slept soundly.

# CHAPTER 5

Every high school has that one couple who everyone agrees is the perfect couple. Nadine's high school was no exception. Tommy Ward and Rebecca Tolliver were that couple. Tommy was the high school football quarterback. For four straight years, he won the state's most valuable player award. Every major university in the country offered him athletic scholarships.

Not only was he a great athlete, he was also a leader. Since his freshman year, he served as class president. No one dared run against him because all his classmates agreed they wanted him to be their president and no one else. Year after year, teachers tried to recruit candidates to run against him but without success.

To add to his list of credits, Tommy was both smart and handsome. His Science Fair projects in forensic science won high praise from the judges at the state Science Fair for four straight years, but perhaps his greatest assets were his movie star good looks and his personality. His six-foot-three-inch frame and handsome appearance commanded attention when he entered a room, but it was his easy going, affable personality that entranced women and won the respect of men who wondered how such a nice guy like Tommy off the field could be such an aggressive *wild-man* on the field: a mystery none of them ever solved.

If Tommy had the women entranced with his good looks, Rebecca raised the fronts of every male young and old upon whom she deigned to bestow her gaze. Her regal appearance with her blonde hair gracefully flowing with every step she took combined with awe-inspiring hip movements made male hearts flutter, but beauty wasn't her only asset. She had a high-powered singing voice that enabled her to sing country, rock, and light opera: a talent that won the admiration of judges who showered her with awards and audiences who rewarded her with long and loud standing ovations.

Girls and older women admired her sense of fashion. Her hour-glass figure extolled the virtues of every garment she wore whether it was a pair of jeans, a skirt, or an expensive evening gown. Girls dieted in a futile effort to attain her figure, they copied the clothes she wore and her hairstyles, but there was only one Rebecca Tolliver. The others were just cheap imitations.

Beauty and singing weren't Rebecca's only assets. She was smart. Since her freshman year, she served as student council president, editor of the yearbook, and had a straight A average in every subject. Her closest competitor in the grade's race was Tommy. She liked to tease him he would never match her grades. That gave her a feeling of superiority and a sense of power. Something else gave her a sense of power. She knew she had captured Tommy's heart.

Rebecca and Tommy loved each other, and for that reason, everyone assumed they would marry and live happily ever after because they were the perfect couple. When Rebecca and Tommy walked down the hallowed halls of the Bradford Bartholomew High School separately or together, the way parted for them. They were royalty. They ruled the school.

# CHAPTER 6

N adine was putting books in her locker when she heard a snotty voice behind her yell, "Hey, Nadine. Got a date for the prom?

"Screw you, Gary," she replied without turning around.

"You wish."

"Not if you were the last male on the planet."

Tensions were running high in the female population at the Bradford Bartholomew High School as the senior prom rapidly approached. Not one of their boyfriends had asked them. A week before the prom, Goldie Green said angrily, "I've had it up to here," as she waved her hand high over her head. "We girls have been patient long enough. It's time we take things into our own hands." She and Herschel had been a couple for more than two years. She felt comfortable asking him to the prom. When he refused, she was stunned as was the entire female population.

Nadine could have cared less about the prom.  She knew she wasn't going to be asked except for the stupid offer from Gary Diefenbaker.  She listened for months to prom-talk with the girls fussing about their gowns' color and style, how much their gowns would cost, who would have the most expensive gown, who was going with whom, who was going to let their boyfriends go all the way, and lots of other general gossip about hairstyles and shoes.  There was even a rumor the prom might be moved to a later date or even cancelled if the boys didn't hurry up and ask the girls.  *A lot of fuss over nothing,"* Nadine thought to herself.

The unexpected happened on the Tuesday before the Saturday night prom a little after 2:30 in the afternoon.  Nadine was at her locker when she heard loud voices.  Moments later bodies raced past her in the direction of the voices.  Nadine shrugged her shoulders and continued rummaging around in her locker looking for the three dollars she had hidden for an emergency.  The noise slowly drifted toward her until she became part of the crowd and could hear a male voice pleading, "Becky!  Please!  Would you just listen!"

"How dare you call me Becky.  How many fucking times have I told you not to call me that?  Rebecca is my name.  Got that?  And no!  I wouldn't go to the fuckin' prom with you or anybody else not after what you've done.  You've spoiled everything."

"Becky...Rebecca. Listen. Please listen. It was supposed to be a joke."

"Some joke.  I've waited and waited for you to ask me to the prom, but no, Mr. Too Important Quarterback pretends not to know there's a prom Saturday night.  You have no idea how much time, effort, and money have gone into this one evening and...and...YOU!" she screamed in desperation.  "OH!" she exhaled in exasperation.  "I don't ever want to see or hear from you ever again!"  She pushed her way through the crowd, leaving behind a bewildered Tommy who turned to the crowd and shrugged his shoulders.  "Some people can't take a joke," he murmured more to himself than the others.

# CHAPTER 7

The next morning students were told to report to the auditorium so Mrs. Adelman, the school principal, could address the student body. Mrs. Adelman, a usually mild-mannered woman, spoke in an unusually harsh tone of voice. She minced no words about the previous day's events. She severely reprimanded the boys for playing such a cruel joke on the girls, but what surprised everyone was she gave the girls the same severe reprimand who, Mrs. Adelman claimed, had focused on the material aspects of the prom: their dresses, their hairdos and not what the prom was meant to celebrate: the last time everyone in the class would be together before going their separate ways. She concluded her comments with, "It's up to you, the students of this class, to decide the fate of your class: to celebrate in joy the last time all of you will be together or break a seventy-three-year tradition and go your separate ways without so much as a final goodbye to your classmates. The decision is yours."  She stopped speaking, looked directly into the eyes of those seated before her, and in a stern voice, barked, "Report to your homerooms.  Now!"

Students quietly filed out of the auditorium chastened by Mrs. Adelman's words and   returned to their homerooms.  As the day wore on, all eyes turned to Tommy: the only person in the school who could decide whether the prom would be held or not.  "Guys, this isn't my decision.  Do whatever you want," whereupon the guys asked, "What are you going to do?"

"I don't know.  I just don't know," Tommy's handsome face looking more worried than anyone had ever seen.

# CHAPTER 8

Thursday morning, a few minutes before eight, Nadine was headed to class when she saw Tommy coming toward her. "Got a minute?" he asked. She had to admit he looked particularly handsome with that lost look in his eyes.

"Sure. What's up?" she asked flippantly.

"I won't beat around the bush. You know the situation."

"I do."

He took a deep breath, and as he exhaled blurted, "Will you go to prom with me?" He expected her to be excited, but Nadine looked him in the eye for an uncomfortable amount of time. "So, it's come to this," she said slowly. "A joke gone bad, and you and I must pay the price. You, because you've lost Rebecca, at least for the time being, and me, because I'm the butt of the joke. 'Handsome Tommy stuck with frizzy-haired loser Nadine Car.' You know that's what everyone will say," she said matter-of-factly. "In answer to your question, I'll be ready at seven-thirty and don't bring a corsage or anything else. This is a business arrangement. Nothing more than that. Understand?"

Tommy hung his head low. "Yes," he replied meekly, disappointed his invitation hadn't been met with gushing enthusiasm but had been reduced to nothing more than a business arrangement.

# CHAPTER 9

Tommy's prom invitation hadn't been a surprise to Nadine. She realized he was in a lose-lose situation. All the pretty girls already had boyfriends who would ask them to the prom so there were only a few leftovers like herself from which he could chose and chose he must because he wouldn't want to go down in school history or in the memory of his classmates, that he, the class president, had killed a seventy-three-year tradition: the senior prom. She also realized when she stared into his eyes, he had momentarily lost his self-confidence. She had read his mind. He feared he would lose face if word ever got out frizzy-haired Nadine Car had rejected him. He would be the laughingstock of the school and maybe the whole town. She couldn't and wouldn't let that happen to Tommy.

At dinner that night, Nadine revealed to her parents that Tommy Ward had asked her to the prom. Both were shocked and pleased he had asked their daughter until Nadine swore them to secrecy. Then she explained what had happened with regard to Rebecca Tolliver, the possible cancellation of the prom, Mrs. Adelman's admonitions, and that she was nothing more than a third-rate booby prize. She also confided she told Tommy this was a business arrangement and nothing more.

"All that said, dear parents, I have a most unusual request to make. Would both of you please stay in a hotel until a few minutes before seven-thirty Saturday night. Tommy's coming at seven-thirty. I want you to meet him."

Her parents looked at each other. Each saw in the other's eyes the answer. With smiling faces and no questions asked, her father turned to his wife and said, "Helen, let's pack our things. We're going to stay in a hotel."

# CHAPTER 10

"Nadine, it's us, Mommy and Daddy."

"I'll be out in a sec."

"That's the doorbell. Do you want me to answer it or do you want to do it yourself?" her mother asked in a raised voice.

"Would you please answer it, Mommy?"

Nadine's mother opened the door. There stood Tommy Ward: movie star handsome. "Tommy?" Mrs. Car gasped.

"Yes, ma'am. I'm here to pick up Nadine for the prom," he said unenthusiastically.

"Nadine. Tommy's here."

"Okay, Mommy, I'm just about ready."

Tommy stood in the doorway. He had prepared himself for the worst: that she would wear one of her weird dresses with those horrible black frame glasses and that damn frizzy hair would tickle his nose when they danced: if she even knew how to dance. He reconciled himself to the fact it was going to be a long evening: one that would go down in his dating annals not just as a flop but a complete disaster: one he would never, ever repeat no matter the circumstances.

He had his own plan. He would dump her as soon as the dance was over, meet up with a few of his buds, and down brewskies till he was drunk as a skunk. He deserved that much. Nevertheless, Nadine's last words that all this prom meant to her was a business deal played repeatedly in his thoughts. Those two words hurt. *She should be damn glad I asked her,* he rationalized. *Business deal hell. The only business deal I want is pussy, and if I can't have that, I might as well get drunk. Screw her.* He shuttered at the thought.

As he stood in the doorway feeling like a total idiot, he took stock of Mr. and Mrs. Car. He could see where Nadine got her no-looks from. They were plain: nice people: but plain: as was the apartment: plain.

"Nadine, dear, Tommy's waiting to take you to the prom." Mrs. Car stood by the open door nervously fidgeting with her fingers waiting for her daughter to appear.

"Another sec or two, Mommy, and I'll be ready." Tommy had high hopes she would stay in her room the rest of the evening, but he knew he couldn't be that lucky.

# CHAPTER 11

The unmistakable sound of an opening door and the click of high heels on hardwood floors gave notice Nadine's arrival was imminent. Tommy held his breath knowing full well he was about to witness a train wreck. All he could envision was frizzy hair and black-frame glasses. Her parents stood quietly not knowing what to expect.

When Nadine entered the living room and walked toward Tommy and her parents, she could see surprise on their faces. No one said a word. The silence was finally broken when Tommy exclaimed, "Holy shit," two words he slowly drew out. He immediately apologized to the Cars for his bad language, but they hadn't heard a word he said. They were in a state of shock: their eyes transfixed on a daughter they didn't recognize.

The frizzy hair had been replaced with an elegant European hairstyle. The glasses were nowhere to be seen as were the brown contacts. Her blue eyes shined brightly, accented by properly groomed eyebrows and curled eyelashes. Her makeup highlighted the contours of her face as well as her perfect nose and sumptuous lips to which a dark red lipstick had been applied.  Her dress, a strapless black mini that left no doubt about the size of her breasts, accented all her curves while the stiletto heels gave added height that emphasized her physical attributes.  In Tommy's eyes, she was the perfect female package.

# CHAPTER 12

Nadine looked at Tommy and in soft, low voice said, "I'm ready." He didn't answer. Nadine's transformation had not only blindsided him but had completely overwhelmed him. He didn't know what to say or how to act. His legs felt rubbery and his feet felt rooted to the floor. Nadine smiled at her parents who were unable to do anything more than stare a wild-eyed stare disbelieving what their eyes told them to be true.

"I'm ready," she said again.

"Yes," he finally managed.

When they arrived at the car, Tommy looked longingly at Nadine and said, "Let's skip the dance."

"This is a business arrangement, remember?" she said sweetly, smiling a smile that further melted Tommy's heart. "To fulfill the contract, you must go to the dance. The king must be seen by his subjects otherwise the prom won't be a success." She smiled once again: this time a smile of encouragement.

As Tommy maneuvered the car through the neighborhood streets, he realized Nadine was right, but that didn't stop him from casting furtive glances at her breasts that resided within the confines of the tight-fitting black dress. He imagined the softness of the skin and the firmness of the breasts in his hands: the protruding nipples in his mouth. His hands perspired and his cock half-hardened in anticipation.

The hotel came into view. Nadine turned to him and said, "There's one last part of the contract I haven't discussed with you yet."

Tommy looked at her not knowing what to expect. "When we go into the hotel, you are to introduce me as Émilie Anjou. Don't worry if you can't pronounce the name correctly. You are to say I'm from another school: a school you refuse to divulge because you don't want the others to know where you found me. You are also to tell them my English is not very good because I have just arrived from France. I will take it from there. This way no one will ever know you asked Nadine Car to the prom."

"I don't care if they know you're Nadine Car."

"To save *your* reputation, silly," she whispered in such a beguiling manner that Tommy had no choice except to accept whatever she said.

# CHAPTER 13

When Tommy and Émilie entered the ballroom hand-in-hand, the assembled crowd cheered wildly. A smiling Vincent Sinclair, vice president of the class, bowed to his king and then to Émilie. He escorted them to a raised platform and motioned for them to sit at their exalted places: two golden thrones. Over one of the thrones, a sign read *King Tommy* and over the other *Queen Rebecca.*

It soon became apparent to everyone in the crowd a serious mistake had been made. Olivia Petrucci took it upon herself to correct it. She jumped up on the platform and took down the sign that read *Queen Rebecca.* Everyone cheered. Then a sudden hush settled over the crowd until a male voice yelled, "Who's the pretty lady, Tommy?"

Tommy stared wild-eyed at his subjects unable to say a word. "Come on Tommy! Don't be shy. Who is she?" an unknown voice shouted from the crowd. Under so much pressure, Tommy remained speechless. He had forgotten her French name. His silence spurred the crowd to chant, "Who is she? Who is she?"

Émilie stood. The crowd hushed, waiting to hear her voice. In French accented English, she spoke slowly. "Me… name…is…Émilie…Anjou. Me…*anglais*…is…is not guut. I… want…thank Tomee…*pour* …*pour*…" It was at this moment the French teacher, Monsieur Levesque, jumped onto the platform and began conversing with Émilie in French. Once she had replied, Levesque translated she was pleased to be asked by Tommy to attend such an event and that she had no idea she would sit on such a high place. He turned and fired off several more questions that she answered forthwith. "She says she lives in a suburb of Paris. I thought I detected a Parisian accent, and she has only been in this country a short time."

"I…hope…to learn…*anglais* fast…so… I can…have… intercourse…with all of you." The boys in the crowd hooted their approval and yelled, "So do we!" while the girls squealed, "Oh my god! I don't believe it!" Émilie looked bewildered until Levesque translated what she had said. She put her hand over her mouth in mock horror and said, *C'est la vie*," that Levesque translated as "such is life".

Her misstatement won the hearts of the crowd. The band struck up a slow song. The vice president of the class invited King Tommy and Queen Émilie to dance the first dance at the seventy-third annual senior prom. The crowd parted so their king and queen could enter the dance floor. Tommy took her hand hesitantly prompting someone to yell, "She ain't gonna bite ya, Tommy." He smiled and took her into his arms but held her at arm's length. She pulled him close, put her head on his chest, and her arm around his neck. The crowd oohed and aahed as they watched the two dominate the dance floor. When the song had finished, Émilie held his hand until the next song began, and everyone danced at this their last time to be together as a class.

# CHAPTER 14

No one ever doubted Émilie Anjou was not Émilie Anjou especially since the French teacher, Monsieur Levesque, spread the rumor that Émilie obviously came from a very fine family because her French was impeccable and her ideas socially progressive: a political doctrine held by the French elite. After hearing this, everyone in attendance at the prom was in awe. They couldn't get enough of Émilie. They asked question after question with Levesque serving as translator. By the end of the evening, King Tommy had lost his subjects to Queen Émilie.

At midnight, with the band playing *Auld Lang Syne*, couples snuggled together and kissed as the last notes faded into oblivion. The king and queen were no exception. Tommy kissed Émilie gently on the lips, anticipating much more in the hours that lay ahead.

The prom ended. Nadine knew what to expect, and Tommy didn't disappoint.  He drove to a secluded spot all the while asking her a thousand questions about how she had learned to speak French since her grades in Levesque's class had been terrible.  He couldn't get over her sophistication and her knowledge of foreign affairs that had fooled the pompous, arrogant Levesque and everyone else.

Tired of answering his questions, Nadine finally said, "Look, Tommy.  I know why we're here so could we dispense with all the questions and get down to business."  She took his hand in hers and looked into his eyes.  Without another word, she leaned across the center console and kissed him gently, then deeply. After a series of deep kisses, she leaned back and lowered her mini to expose her breasts. Tommy gazed upon their beauty. His vision had come true. He leaned over the center console and gently took her left breast in his left hand.  The skin was creamy white and soft while the breast itself was firm to the touch.  He leaned lower so he could put its nipple in his mouth: his tongue gently caressing it.  Nadine groaned with ecstasy: an ecstasy she did not feel.

Three things surprised her: her lack of interest in his attention to her breasts, his intense interest in them, and her lack of interest in him.  She endured his caressing, kissing, licking, squeezing, and sucking the nipples of her ample breasts for as long as she could but enough was enough.  She gently removed the nipple of her right breast from his mouth and raised his sweating head so she could lift her mini above her waist to reveal she wasn't wearing panties.

"Holy shit," Tommy breathlessly uttered seeing her dark pubic hairs.  Without hesitation, he maneuvered himself over the center console and gear shift, so his mouth was opposite her opening.  Her sweet smell intoxicated him.  He breathed long and deep before he placed his eager tongue in her opening.  He breathed in heavy gasps as he moved his tongue back and forth, up and down, and side-to-side.

Suddenly he jumped back over the console.  "Oh shit.  I gonna fuckin' cum."  He unbuckled his pants, shoved his pants and boxer shorts to his ankles, and raised his shirt to his neck. Nadine reached over with her left hand and put it around his hard penis.  Seconds later, his body jerked uncontrollably.  "I'm cumming.  I'm fuckin' cumming," he wheezed as hot streams of white liquid gushed from his cock over his chest, face, and hair. When the jerking subsided, he looked at her, grinned a silly grin proud of the load he had just discharged and said, "I've been savin' up for a long time: like two weeks."

"I see."

He reached into the center console and took out a package of tissues.  Nadine took his hand with the tissues and whispered in a sweet French accent, "Let me do that for you."  She gently cleaned his body and hair with tissue after tissue, kissing him from-time-to-time as she did so.  He lay back in the seat happy and content.

When she completed the task, she pulled down her mini to cover her opening and raised the upper part to cover her exposed breasts.  She looked at him.  He was at peace with the world: his eyes closed: his breathing normal.  In a matter-of-fact voice, she said, "Show's over.  It's late and I'm tired.  Take me home, then you can meet up with your buddies, brag how you screwed the French girl, and get drunk out of your mind."

"No, Émilie, Nadine.  I don't want that.  I wanna stay here with you.  I wanna do it all again."

"Not to be, Tommy.  Remember, this was a business deal: nothing personal.  I have fulfilled my part of the bargain. I consider our deal consummated.  Now take me home," she said coldly.

# CHAPTER 15

The moment Nadine got home she removed all vestiges of Émilie. She had been careful to choose a hairstyle that hadn't changed the length of her hair so it was easy to wash out the coloring of the European hairstyle and regain her natural brownish-blonde hair and frizzy-look with little effort. While she did these things, she reviewed the night's events. The hairstyle, the makeup, and the black mini she had altered from an old dress hanging in the closet had been a success. She was pleased her French held up, fooling Levesque who gave her a D- her sophomore year. She never expected Tommy to freeze before his adoring fans. Nevertheless, she was pleased she had the good sense to introduce herself and had teased the crowd, especially the boys, with her intercourse joke.

Her lack of sexual gratification with the so-called perfect male did concern her. If she felt nothing with him, would she ever feel anything with anybody? She dismissed the thought as unimportant and focused on the other events of the evening that had been a tremendous success. What gave her the biggest thrill was she had been in control the entire evening from the time Tommy picked her up until he took her home. This gave her the confidence to move to the next phase of her plan.

# CHAPTER 16

Nadine's parents returned home Sunday afternoon. They were shocked and dismayed to see the old, frizzy-haired Nadine had returned, but that wasn't to be their only shock. After a few minutes of idle prom conversation, Nadine informed her parents she intended to leave them and their home: forever.

"What?" her mother screamed in dismay. "Where will you go? What will you do? What will you use for money? How will you live?" she asked in rapid-fire succession.

"Don't worry, Mother, I'll be fine," Nadine answered in a calm voice. "There is one other thing I must tell you. Once I'm gone, you will never hear from me again. I will never write or phone. You must never try to contact me. I appreciate all you've done for me the last eighteen years. Now it's time for me to leave."

Her mother cried out, "You're my only child.  I'll never have any grandchildren."

"No, you won't," Nadine said coldly.

Her father seeing the determination in Nadine's eyes asked, "How soon will you leave?"

"I'm not sure, but one day I'll be gone, and when I am, don't call the police or file a missing person's claim."

"Nadine, how can you do this to your mother and father: your parents?"

"Mother, you don't get it.  You and my father have done a wonderful job taking care of me.  I thank you for that.  Now it's time for me to be on my own. You should celebrate that I'm leaving: that I'm ready to begin a new life."

"But what about college and all our plans?" her mother pleaded more than asked.

"Those are your plans: not mine.  I have things to do so I'm going to kiss you both one last time."  She kissed each on their cheeks.  She felt no remorse for what she was about to do. What she did feel was a new sense of freedom.

# CHAPTER 17

Nadine's cell phone rang. "Thomas," she said sharply into the phone. "I don't know how you got this number, but never use it again."

"Émilie…"

"Never, ever call me that again. Promise me you'll never say that name again."

"I promise," came a weak reply.

"Good. Now we understand each other."

"It's you who doesn't understand. I'm in a helluva jam here. My phone's been ringin' since I got home early this morning. I haven't been to bed with everyone callin'. The guys are goin' nuts. They fell in love with you: just like me. They wanna know what school you go to, where you live. They wanna know everything about you. Some of the guys have trolled every social media site they can think of searching for you. They've even researched your last name and are looking for your relatives in France. This thing is totally out of control, and there's nothing I can do to stop it."

"That's your problem, Thomas. Not mine. Take my advice and go back to Rebecca and live happily ever after. I'm going now."

"No! Wait! I've been thinkin'. Every university that's offered me a scholarship says I can bring my girlfriend, and they'll give her a full four-year scholarship."

"Not interested."

"But I love you."

"You paid no attention to me since kindergarten. Now you're suddenly in love with me? All you care about is some figment of your imagination. How shallow you are, Thomas. Grow up!" She pressed the *end call* button.

The following morning the Car's doorbell rang. "Who is it?" Nadine asked through the closed door.

"It's me, Tommy."

"Go away and never come back."

"Nadine! Don't talk like that. I love you. I want to be with you: for always."

"Okay, Thomas.  You asked for it."  She opened the door to expose her frizzed-hair, black-framed glasses, brown contacts, and a shapeless, purple dress.  "Is this what you love?  Is this who you want to be with the rest of your life, because this is me, the real me.  Now leave me alone."  She slammed the door in his face.

"Nadine," she heard him sob.  "Why do you make it so hard?"

She didn't answer.  She went to her bedroom and packed a few necessities.  When her parents returned from work, she was gone.

# CHAPTER 18

Ever since Nadine was a little girl, her parents had given her a few dollars for birthdays and Christmases: not that they weren't generous but because they were saving money for her future.  Nadine prized those few dollars because they gave her a sense of freedom.  By the time she was ten, she decided she wanted to be rich, not just rich, but fabulously rich, and she didn't want to work for some crummy company like her father locked up in a room adding numbers. She wanted the easy life: free to travel and do as she pleased.

To fulfill this dream, she conducted meticulous computer research. One of her searches involved finding a virtual currency that suited her needs.  For months, she had no luck until she accidentally came across a business blog that mentioned a virtual currency known only to a few called Crypto-Coin organized and managed by world-wide crime syndicates.  The fact that it was a criminal enterprise intrigued Nadine.  With her highly developed computer skills, it didn't take long to locate and hack into the Crypto-Coin site. This drew the immediate attention of the members of the Crypto-Coin community. They considered their site secure, and since no one had ever hacked it, they weren't just concerned about their cyber security but intrigued as to who could have done it.

Impressed as the CC community was, they couldn't trust this unknown cyber hacker. They reasoned that maybe the hack was nothing more than pure luck, but more important, they had to be certain this wasn't some sort of legal entrapment. They needed to test this individual further to be certain he-she was on the up-and-up. The CC community decided to construct various tests that were challenging but ones that wouldn't trigger police attention in case the person was legit.

Nadine was pleased someone at Crypto-Coin had taken an interest because she considered CC her road to riches. There were four aspects of the currency that appealed to her. The name Crypto-Coin: crypto meaning hidden and secret: fascinated her because it appealed to her sense of danger. She liked the anonymity it offered since no one in the organization would ever know her name or identity. She liked that it could be used in thousands of legitimate businesses worldwide such as airlines, apartment and car rentals, hotels, restaurants, and easily converted into cash, but what intrigued her the most was it was part of a worldwide underground network of criminal organizations whose motto was "Solve the Impossible", CC's way of saying outsmart the world's legal and governmental systems.

She loved the challenge of the tests and solved every one of the complex cyber-problems. After a year of such tests, the CC community decided the individual who had hacked their site was worthy of membership: a privilege that allowed the unknown individual to invest money in the Crypto-Coin Bank and to avail himself-herself of all its businesses and services.

# CHAPTER 19

Once Nadine was accepted into the Crypto-Coin community, she wasted no time in buying crypto-currency with the few dollars her parents had given her for Christmases and birthdays. Those few dollars, due to CC's incredible interest rate, had soared in value, so when she departed her parents' apartment, she had more than enough money to embark on her new career as an appropriator: a word she used to describe the transition of funds from one person's account to her own.

She flew to Chicago to meet with a locksmith who, upon request, had made a special key. When she entered the locksmith's shop on Chicago's south-side, a middle-aged black man looked at her quizzically since he didn't have many white customers let alone one so young. She gave the proper CC code with her cell phone whereupon the man reached under the counter and put a key in her left hand. She immediately left the shop.  Once outside, she pretended she had made a mistake, shrugged her shoulders in frustration, and gave the impression she had been given the wrong address.

Nadine smiled when she got back to the hotel and looked at the key: the key to her success.  To her surprise, it looked no different than any other key for unlocking doors, but she hoped it could do much more than that.  She was eager to try it out, but first she had to search social media to decide which lucky associate, as she called her intended victims, would be her first associate.  She was in the bathroom sitting on the toilet when she heard the alarm on her cell phone.  She immediately got up, ran to the phone, and enabled the crypto-warning where she saw the words *LEAVE NOW!*

# CHAPTER 20

Nadine gathered up the few things she had taken out of her suitcase, flung them back in the case, and slowly walked out of the hotel so as not to attract attention. Once on the street, she activated her CC account with *Need Car* followed by *Need Safe House*. Instructions immediately came up on her cell phone: *Cadillac Escalade: Illinois Plate AXQ3749S.* Four minutes later a Cadillac Escalade approached. She checked the plate number. The Escalade with blacked out windows came to a halt in front of her. The rear door slid open. She got in. A darkened partition separated her from the driver and blackened windows kept her from seeing outside. A recorded voice commanded, "Place all electronic devices in the box located under seat. Failure to do so will cancel this trip." Nadine did as she was directed.

Many minutes later, the car tilted forward as if going down a steep hill. It stopped. She heard the click of the door unlocking. An older woman opened the door and said quietly, "Follow me." Nadine got out of the Escalade and followed the woman through a door to an elevator that took them to an undisclosed floor. She followed the woman down a hallway to an apartment. Once inside the apartment, the woman smiled and said, "Welcome."

Nadine sighed relief. For the first time in her life, she had been frightened: not startled like when her father came into her bedroom late at night, but heart-pumping scared she would be arrested and her life as an appropriator would end before it started. The older woman offered Nadine something to eat and drink, but she was too stressed to have anything.

"First things first," the older woman said in a calm voice so as not to further frighten Nadine. "I need to apprise you of the situation you're in. A few minutes after you left the locksmith's, the Chicago police arrested the man who owns the shop. We have known for some time the police have been taping everyone going in and out of the shop. However, we have friends at the police department who will make sure the tape never sees the light of day. Nevertheless, the police most certainly will want to question you as to why you were in a black neighborhood on the southside of Chicago, why you were on a back-street like Crocker, and why you went into that particular shop. That's the basic situation. However, there is one other problem: your hairstyle. It makes you easy to identify. That's why you're here."

The woman could see fear in Nadine's face. "But not to worry. All's not lost. We can change your hairstyle and get you new clothes, but enough about business. You must be tired. Let me take you to your room. There's a white fleece robe laid out on the bed. Please remove your clothes and put on the robe. When you've done this, place your clothes outside the door plus your suitcase and everything in it. We must discard everything so the police can't trace you."

Nadine was tired, yet her mind couldn't rest. Thomas's coming to the apartment had upset her plans. She should have changed her hairstyle, she should have used CC air transport instead of a regular airline, but she had so many things on her mind. Besides, who would have thought she would walk into a police raid at a locksmith's shop? Nevertheless, these were serious mistakes: ones she didn't intend to repeat.

# CHAPTER 21

When Nadine opened the bedroom door, she saw the woman sitting in a chair texting. "Have a good rest?" the woman asked when Nadine entered the room and sat in a chair opposite her.

"I've had better."

"I see you changed your hairstyle."

"Something I should have done sooner."

"Most definitely," the woman said unsympathetically. "Now to business. Your old clothes have been disposed of. New ones have arrived. Before we eat breakfast, there are a few things I have to tell you. Unfortunately, none of them good. First, the news about you. It seems the police were ready to arrest the locksmith when you arrived. They had to wait until you left to follow through with the arrest. They couldn't hold you at the time because that would have compromised the arrest plus the fact you were in the shop less than thirty seconds.

"The tape has revealed the owner of the shop put something in your left hand.  I must ask you to give me whatever the locksmith gave you.  I'll return it when you leave."  Reluctantly Nadine reached into the robe's pocket and handed her the key.

"As for the police," the woman continued, "our informant tells us they checked the airlines and found a Marjorie Gibbons who fit your description.  However, since you're a minor and committed no crime, the police will pursue your case no further.  One other lucky break.  The informant tells us the tape does not clearly show your face while you were in the shop because of the shop's dirty windows.  Sometimes it pays to be dirty."  The woman smiled.  Nadine didn't.  "I trust Marjorie Gibbons is a pseudonym?" the woman asked changing the subject.

Nadine nodded her head *yes*.

"There's one other thing.  It seems you peed in a toilet and neglected to flush."

"Oh," Nadine said hesitantly thinking over past events.  "That's when I got the alert."

"I see.  The police will run your urine through some DNA tests.  Not to worry.  The bacteria in urine quickly disintegrates the DNA.  The most they can learn is your sex and your approximate age: two things they already know.”

“I guess I’ve made lots of mistakes,” Nadine said contritely.

“Yes, you have,” the woman said without sympathy. “Unfortunately, I have more bad news.  Yesterday, the FBI arrested four CC members.  Why, we can’t be certain, nor can we be certain if the arrests will continue.  CC’s satellites and communication networks are presently inactive but still intact. The disruptions will be short-lived, but under the circumstances, it’s been decided you stay here until things stabilize.”

# CHAPTER 22

The last thing Nadine wanted was to stay in an unfamiliar apartment with an unfamiliar woman. She wanted her freedom and not have this woman or anyone else control her life. She thought long and hard about her choices until she realized she had no choices. She had to stay where she was. "I'll stay," she informed the woman.

"Good. Now we need to call each other a name. Please call me Betty, and if it's all right with you, I'll call you by your pseudonym, Marjorie."

"Sounds like a plan," Nadine answered unenthusiastically.

Betty reminded Nadine of a kind, gentle grandmother with her salt and pepper hair. She guessed Betty was in her early to mid-fifties. She appreciated her kindness, trying to be as hospitable as possible under the circumstances, but she worried Betty hadn't returned her cell phone. "What about my cell phone?" she asked.

"Your phone's been destroyed.  When it's time for you to leave, I'll give you a new one and put you back on the CC network."  She smiled a broad, warm smile meant to reassure Nadine all was well.

Days turned into a week.  Nadine became restless but said nothing.  A week turned into two weeks: then a month.  Each day Nadine became increasingly restless.  She wanted to run but couldn't.  She had no cell phone, no CC connections, no money.  She had to stay put.

Betty, realizing Nadine was becoming increasingly restless, assured her it wasn't safe for her to leave the apartment.  "Police have arrested hundreds of CC members.  Be patient, my dear.  Things look bad now, but they'll get better."  She smiled a grandmotherly smile meant to calm a nervous teenager.

The combination of Betty's smile and bad news surprisingly served to calm Nadine's nerves.

# CHAPTER 23

Crypto-Coin board members decided there was only one possible individual responsible for so many arrests of their members: the cyber hacker. Nadine had no idea she was being held captive while IT specialists tracked her every cell phone call and Internet search. If they found she had ever contacted local or federal law-enforcement-agencies, the CC board instructed Betty to liquidate her.

Nadine's patience came to an end. She had enough of being caged like an animal. "I'm splitting," she informed Betty in a snotty voice one morning after breakfast, "and there's nothing you can do about it." She moved toward the door.

"Stop! Right now!" Betty commanded, but Nadine continued toward the door. She felt her body being jerked backward as Betty pushed past her and blocked the way. Nadine tried to force her way past Betty, but Betty gave her two nasty surprises. She had a body of steel and was an expert in the martial arts. Nadine's thin body bounced off Betty's who grabbed her arm and flung her across the room. Nadine staggered backward and fell onto the sofa. Stunned, she regrouped forces and lunged at Betty who flung her back onto the sofa.

"Look, little bitch. Let's get this straight. You're here until I release you. Got that? And if by some fluke you ever get past me, you won't make it to the elevator alive. So no more nonsense. You'll do what you're told and like it."

Betty pulled Nadine from the sofa, shoved her into the bedroom, and locked the door. Nadine threw herself on the bed where she evaluated her situation. It was grim at best. She was no match for Betty's superior strength. Betty controlled her. Worse yet, there was no hope of escape or rescue.

# CHAPTER 24

The sound of a key in the lock, the click of the lock's opening were the sounds that roused Nadine. Two men wearing ski masks approached the bed. One man blindfolded her while the other dragged her out of bed, pushed her out of the apartment into the waiting elevator. When the elevator doors opened, one of the men pushed her forward. Several spin arounds and a hard shove sent her reeling out of control. She fell. She heard a door slam shut and three locks snap into place.

She removed the blindfold and struggled to her feet. As she did so, she heard the gritty sounds of minute stone particles rubbing against the rough cement floor. One lone bulb hanging from an electrical cord cast just enough light for her to make out her surroundings: a cot that contained a small, yellow-stained pillow and a badly frayed blanket. Next to the cot was a half-used roll of toilet paper and a hole beside it.

She sank onto the cot: alone: lost. She could hold back the tears no more. She sobbed.

# CHAPTER 25

The echoing sounds of three opening locks intruded on Nadine's nightmarish dreams. She heard the door open, and something slide over the gritty floor. The door closed and the three locks snapped back into place. Hesitantly, she got up from the cot and guided by the aromas of hot food made her way toward it. She had no idea how long she had last eaten, but she was hungry despite the hostile surroundings.

She found a tray that contained fresh fruit and hot food: apples, oranges, bananas, grapes, roast beef in gravy, French fries, and salad smothered in balsamic vinaigrette. She looked for silverware but there was none: not even a napkin. She would have to eat with her hands. She reached for an apple and began eating it greedily along with juicy, red grapes. She heard the key in the lock. She quickly hid a banana under the pillow and waited for the three locks to snap open.

Two men wearing ski masks and goggles entered the room. One slammed her flat on the floor and pinned down her neck with his foot while the other removed the tray. Moments later, the man took his foot from her neck, the door closed, and the three locks snapped shut. When she got up, she felt under the pillow for the banana. It was gone replaced with a note: *You stole. You will be punished.* Moments later the dim light went dark.

# CHAPTER 26

As Nadine lay on the cot in the darkened room, she realized her captors were going to use food and drink to control her: that she had fallen into their trap by hiding the banana. Why else was a note placed on the cot, not scribbled in haste, but neatly written. She smiled. Yes, she had made a mistake, but they too had made a mistake. As she saw it, the score was even.

Her thoughts turned to why she was being held captive. She grabbed the sides of the cot when she realized CC considered her the snitch who had not only hacked their site but had betrayed them. Her heart sank as the reality of the situation sank in: that this black nothingness could be her grave.

# CHAPTER 27

The thought of dying in the black nothingness brought uncontrollable panic. Nadine struggled for each breath. Then something strange happened. She slowly became aware of a new tranquility. She realized she hadn't done this alone: that there was a force stronger than she, not some god, but the mind. The mind made her feel stronger: that she wasn't alone: that the mind was there to help her through this experience: that the mind was in control. Nevertheless, she could feel her temperature rise as the body consumed vital fat and moisture reserves needed to preserve life. Thirst threatened to close her windpipe. She fought for every drop of saliva to slacken her intense thirst. She knew she didn't have long to live under these conditions. She barely weighed a hundred pounds. Unconsciousness became her friend as she lapsed in and out of it waiting for the inevitable.

# CHAPTER 28

Through the haze of semi-consciousness, Nadine vaguely heard three locks snap open one-by-one, something being placed over her eyes, and being helped up from the cot. Her weakened legs gave out. She collapsed into a numb void.

When she awoke, she found herself in the same bedroom when she had first arrived. She felt clean. Her hair was damp. A fresh-smelling fleece robe warmed her. She lay staring at the ceiling when Betty came into the room carrying a tray. "This is your breakfast," she said coldly as she placed the breakfast tray over Nadine's legs. "Eat slowly so you don't throw it up. You'll find a barf bag on the tray. If you feel ill, be certain to use it."

The sight and smell of food made Nadine sick to her stomach. She forced herself to take a bite of buttered toast. She could barely swallow it. Her stomach felt as if it were tied in a knot. She had never been a coffee drinker, but with several packets of sugar and numerous containers of rich cream, it tasted like the elixir of life.  With something warm in her stomach, she lay back on the soft, warm bed and fell into a deep sleep.

She awoke to the sickening smells of hot food.  Betty set the tray on a table and said unemotionally, "Lunchtime." Having delivered the tray, she opened the drapes to let in the pale sunshine and left the room.

Nadine got up from the bed and went into the bathroom where she looked in the mirror.  She didn't recognize her emaciated face.  She looked like a druggie or someone dying of an incurable disease: hair cut short, skin a lifeless grayish-white, dark circles under the eyes.  She looked more like an old lady than a girl of eighteen.

She returned to the tray on the table.  She wanted to eat something, but the sight of food sickened her.  She returned to the bed and snuggled under the covers while the mind struggled to recover from the traumatic past events.  It took a while for it to calm itself before she could rest.

Betty awakened her for dinner.  After she finished the sugar and cream-filled coffee, she fell back on the pillow and drifted into a sound sleep.  The next morning Betty brought her a food laden tray and coldly commanded, "Eat your breakfast. Clothes are hanging on a hook in the bathroom.  Change into them.  You'll be leaving in an hour so don't tarry."

# CHAPTER 29

The SUV with darkened windows came to a stop. A two-tone chime sounded waking Nadine from her semi-conscious state. The sliding door opened. A pleasant female voice said, "Please exit vehicle." Nadine did as the voice commanded. The sliding door closed and the vehicle sped off.

As the SUV disappeared into the distance, Nadine surveyed her new surroundings: a drug-infested neighborhood. She looked like the emaciated homeless men sitting on the cold sidewalk leaning against the cement wall except she was wearing a pink sweatshirt and hoodie that clearly identified her as female.

She decided the safest place was the double yellow line in the middle of the nearly deserted street so she could be as far away from the crazies as possible. She knew she wouldn't be there for long: just long enough to connect to her CC account for the money she so badly needed. Teeth chattering and hands shaking from the cold, she reached into the inside pocket of the hoodie and much to her surprise felt the key. She smiled. Having the key made her feel stronger: more in control. She reached into another pocket and found a cell phone. Betty had lived up to her word. She had connected the new cell phone to the CC network. Nadine activated her CC bank account where she found the following message: *Funds on hold. Reconnect nearest CC Bank.*

The nearest CC bank was eight blocks away. With no money, she had no choice. She had to walk and to make matters worse, walk directly into a fierce, icy-cold wind. Her diminished weight and strength made it difficult to walk against a wind that was determined to impede her forward progress.

The walk seemed never-ending, but finally she saw the bank on the other side of the busy street. To Nadine, in the condition she was in, it seemed like an impenetrable barrier. A well-dressed man, seeing her shaking badly, asked her where she was going. She pointed to the bank across the street. He gently took her arm and led her to the other side. She turned to say something to him, but all she saw was the man's back as he continued on his way.

When she arrived at the bank's entrance, she didn't have the strength to move the heavy revolving door. It wasn't until a woman leaving the bank pushed it around that she was able to enter. Once inside the warm bank, she sat on a bench in the lobby to regain whatever strength she could. When she felt strong enough, she activated her CC bank code. A man dressed in a suit appeared and motioned to follow him. In his oak-paneled office, she typed in the amount she wanted. The man counted out in one-hundred-dollar bills the amount she asked for and placed them in an envelope. He then gave her a second envelope.

Nadine left the office and sat down on the same bench as before. She opened the second envelope and saw her account had grown substantially while she had been in captivity. Betty had been right about one thing. Things were getting better. She scanned the CC network for a list of hotels. She found one that suited her needs. She called Uber and by the time she managed to get through the revolving door, the car was waiting.

# CHAPTER 30

The clerk at the hotel's check-in desk yelled, "Get the hell out of here and stay out. I don't want your kind in here," when he saw the emaciated Nadine approaching him. He quickly changed his mind when she activated her CC code. "Oh, well, that's different," he stammered. "Please sign the register," he said in his official hotel tone of voice.

Nadine signed the register as Rebecca Tolliver. "Welcome to the Cozy Arms, Miss, ah, Miss." He turned the register around so he could see her last name. "Tolliver. And how long will you be with us?"

"I don't…" Without warning, Nadine fainted, falling to the floor in a heap of pinkness. The long walk in the icy-cold sapped what little strength she had. The clerk ran from behind the desk, called to one of the porters, picked her up, and carried her to Room 827. The porter opened the door to 827 with the house card so the clerk could lay her down on the bed.  "Thank you," she murmured.

Realizing there was nothing more they could do, the clerk and porter quietly left the room.  After the clerk shut the door, he turned to the porter and said, "Whatever she's got, she ain't gonna get over it."  The porter nodded in agreement.

# CHAPTER 31

It was midafternoon when Nadine awoke. She was surprised to see she was fully clothed, including her shoes. She smiled a tired smile at the thought she had been so exhausted she hadn't taken off her shoes.

Stomach pains had wakened her. She was hungry, yet the thought of food sickened her. Nevertheless, she knew she had to put something into her body. She scanned the hotel menu on the table next to the bed. An asterisk at the top of the menu stated room service was no longer available. She reached into her hoodie pocket and pulled out her cell phone. She activated her CC code and found a nearby twenty-four-hour coffee-shop.

"Hello?" Nadine said into the cell phone as forcefully as she could. "Do you deliver?"

"Nah," the gruff voice replied. "Too much trouble. Wait a sec. Here's my wife. She takes care of that kinda stuff."

"Yes?" said a more pleasant-sounding voice.

Nadine explained she was staying at the Cozy Arms Hotel, that she was recuperating from cancer, and that she needed delivery to her room since she didn't have the strength to come to the restaurant.

"Oh, you poor, dear. We most certainly will deliver whatever you need. Just tell us what you want, and we'll deliver it."

"Room..." She paused to look at the card envelope on the table next to the bed. "Room 827, a large coffee with lots of cream and sugar, and the largest container of orange juice you have. Also send a receipt that you have received one-hundred dollars from Rebecca Tolliver." She paused to catch her breath. In a thin, cracked voice, "I realize my request is..." A sudden wave of exhaustion overcame her.

Nadine's frail voice convinced the voice on the other end this was no prank call. "Not to worry, dear," she said in a motherly voice. "We're filling the order right now. Freddie our delivery boy will be there in minutes." Nadine gasped for breath. "You all right, dear?"

"Yes, just a dry throat. Makes talking difficult."

"Freddie is just leaving. He'll be there in a couple of minutes."

"Thanks," Nadine uttered into the cell phone before she collapsed back on the pillow.

# CHAPTER 32

Freddie arrived at Room 827 with a large container of coffee, lots of sugar packets and small containers of cream along with a half-gallon of orange juice. He became concerned when he knocked on the door several times, and there was no answer. He called the front desk. The clerk fearing the worst rushed to the room. After repeated knockings, he used the house card to open the door.

"Jesus," Freddie said aloud when he saw Nadine's emaciated body.

"I'm calling 911," the frightened clerk said as he pulled out his cell phone.

"No!" Nadine gasped. "I've used up my hospital days. No hospital will admit me."

"I mighta known. Damn government rules," the angered clerk replied.

Nadine in a weak voice asked the delivery boy if she could have some orange juice.

"Oh, sure," Freddie replied suddenly feeling needed. He quickly pulled the half-gallon of orange juice from a plastic bag, unscrewed the cap, poured the cold juice into a plastic cup, and placed it in her shaking hands.

She raised her head from the pillow and took several small sips. She smacked her lips in enjoyment. "Good." Exhausted, she handed the cup to Freddie and lay back on the pillow. She remained silent for a few moments before raising her head from the pillow and asked, "Did you bring the receipt?"

"Yes, but it's really not necessary. Mom says…"

"I pay." She slumped back on the pillow. She reached into the inside pocket of the hoodie and took out an envelope. She raised her head from the pillow and took out a single one-hundred-dollar bill. Hands shaking, she handed it to Freddie then fell back on the pillow and slipped into unconsciousness. Freddie placed the receipt on the bed next to her, then he and the clerk left the room. Once in the corridor, the clerk turned to Freddie and whispered, "I had to carry her up here. She couldn't walk by herself. She can't weigh more than fifty pounds."

"Mom says she has cancer."

"Damn! I was afraid of that." The clerk and Freddie walked down the corridor each lost in his own thoughts.

# CHAPTER 33

adine had taken several sips of hot coffee when she heard a soft knock at the door. "Miss Tolliver," came a voice through the door. "It's me, Mrs. Megalos. I'm from the coffee shop. I spoke to you on the phone. Can I come in and speak with you?"

Nadine raised her voice as much as she could and said, "I need…" Her voice gave out.

"Are you all right, Miss Tolliver?" When there was no answer, she said forcefully, "You need a doctor. I'm going to get you one."

Nadine took another swallow of the coffee. It cleared her throat enough so she could answer in a stronger voice. "I have one: my mind. It will heal me."

"What kind of nonsense is that: your mind will heal you," Mrs. Megalos replied angrily. She paused for a few moments and then in a much calmer voice added, "You need someone to be with you: to keep you company.  I can do that."

Nadine wheezed with great effort, "No doctor."

"You're ill.  You need help."

Nadine took another swallow of the hot coffee.  In as nasty a voice as she could muster said, "Go away.  Don't come back.  If you do, I'll leave this hotel."

# CHAPTER 34

Once Nadine finished drinking the coffee Freddie had delivered, she picked up the cell phone and found a store that accepted CC accounts. She ordered flannel pajamas, thermal socks, fleece-lined slippers, and a fleece bathrobe.

An hour later a message appeared on her cell phone that her order had been delivered. When she approached the door, she saw an envelope had been slipped under it. The enclosed note was on hotel stationery. *Miss Tolliver: You may continue your stay at the Cozy Arms as long as you deem it necessary and that all expenses incurred during your stay have been waived. It is the pleasure of this hotel to serve you in any way we can. Thank you for selecting the Cozy Arms for your stay. Sincerely, the Cozy Arms Management and Staff.*

The note stunned Nadine. Forgetting the package that awaited her, she returned to the bed and read the note over and over.  She couldn't decide if this was an apology from CC for the horrific treatment she had suffered or whether the hotel had taken pity on her.  When she tired of the note, she remembered the package.  She slowly made her way to the door.  When she opened it, she found a beautifully wrapped package with a handwritten note slipped under the pink ribbon that read, "We are always at your service."  She smiled at the simple message. It boosted her morale considerably.

# CHAPTER 35

Nadine's original plan had been to stay in the Cozy Arms for two or three weeks and then begin her career as an appropriator. After several days, she became aware she would have to re-evaluate her plans. She was in much worse physical condition than she realized. Her stomach still felt as if it were tied in knots unable to accept food. She searched the Internet for nutritious foods for people who found it difficult to eat solid food. She found a food that appealed to her: ice cream. She hoped it would soothe her stomach and untie the knots. She decided to include a milkshake in her future orders.

To keep her mind active, she decided to calculate how many days she had been in captivity. She checked the hotel's receipt for the date she checked in. She knew when the prom was held and that she left two days later. She calculated she had been in captivity two-hundred-forty days and one-hundred seventy-nine days in the hole. Somewhere in the darkness, she turned nineteen. *Helluva way to spend a birthday,* she thought to herself

# CHAPTER 36

A week passed. Nadine was pleased the milkshakes eased the stomach pains. Now that she felt a bit stronger, she could stop focusing her attention on her health and think about the future.

She weighed her options. She could return home. Her parents would fuss seeing her in her present condition. They would ask a multitude of questions: when, where, why, and how could such a thing have happened to their daughter. She could hear her mother saying over and over, "My, poor baby. My poor, poor baby," while stroking her hair. Her father would try to soothe her mother with comforting words like, "Now, now, Helen. Everything's all right now. She's back home where she belongs, with us, safe and sound. Nothing bad will ever happen to her again," words that would never satisfy her mother because deep in her heart she knew her baby, her only child, her dearest Nadine, would never be safe.

Of course, she would make up outrageous lies to satisfy her parents' questions, and if she got tangled up in her lies, she could always rely on the severity of her injuries that caused her to have mental lapses and moments of confusion.  Once she recovered from her injuries, she would acquiesce to their demands and attend college where she would major in some useless subject, marry some nine-to-five schlub, have children, go to mindless PTA meetings, basketball games, dance recitals, get fat, and die. In Nadine's mind, such a life would be suffocating and useless, but it would be safe.

Or, she could withdraw her money from the CC bank and sever her connections with an organization she no longer trusted because they had blown her cover.  CC knew all about her including distinguishing features of her naked body since either Betty with or without the help of the masked men had showered her.  Through the cell phone, they could trace her every move for the rest of her life, and if they decided to turn her over to the police or return her to captivity, they could do so at a moment's notice.

However, if she dumped CC, she would regain her anonymity and no longer have to fear recapture from a vindictive CC, but she would lose all CC connections and services she worked so hard to establish. She had witnessed the effectiveness of the CC network from warning her to leave the hotel, to transporting her to a safe house, to withdrawing money from a CC bank at a high interest rate, to using CC services like staying in a hotel for free, to buying clothes. If she left CC, she would surrender all these services because no other virtual currency offered such a high interest rate or the multitudinous CC services. She would be on her own with no organization to protect her.

Nadine weighed her options. Just what kind of a life did she want to have: a safe one with nothing but mind-numbing daily-drudgery or a risky one filled with excitement and danger. Did she want to throw away all those years of intense Internet research learning how to disguise herself and to speak foreign languages? She realized her final decision would change her life forever and once made, could never be taken back.

# CHAPTER 37

In Nadine's weakened condition, college, marriage, children, and death seemed like a no-brainer, but as the days passed, she cast aside a life of safe drudgery in favor of a dangerous, risky one filled with excitement. Although still weak and considerably underweight, she decided it was time to search the Internet for her first associate: someone who would be an easy target for her first appropriation. The search excited her. "Yess!" she hissed to herself as numerous possibilities popped up on her cell phone.

Like a hawk swooping down on its prey, she focused on a professor at Purdue University, Chairwoman of the Feminine Humanities and Resource Development Department. She accessed the CC network, entered the woman's name, Anita Pierson, the city in which she lived, and to be sure she had the right Anita Pierson, her occupation. Immediately Pierson's address appeared with photos of her adoring female students along with photos of the exterior and interior of the house. *Thank you, Anita Pierson. You have just made my life a whole lot easier,* Nadine whispered to herself.

Nadine knew she wasn't strong enough to leave the hotel to carry out her first project in person. To amuse herself, she decided to hack Pierson's bank accounts and possibly save herself a trip to Purdue University, but Pierson, ever mindful of potential hackers, had multiple layers of heavily encrypted security that thwarted Nadine's hacking attempts. Nadine decided to give up the exercise when a notice popped up on the screen: *HACKER BEWARE! YOU ARE SUBJECT TO IMMEDIATE ARREST.* She realized it was time to give up hacking and go back to robbing Ms. Pierson the old-fashioned way: up close and in person.

# CHAPTER 38

Nadine had been cooped up in the Cozy Arms Hotel for more than three months which had given her a severe case of cabin fever. She decided it was time to begin her appropriation career. The photos of Pierson had been most revealing. She preferred the biker look: black leather jacket, short black leather skirt, high black leather boots, and a soft, black leather cap with visor. This last item Nadine especially liked because the visor pulled down over her forehead would hide the upper portion of her face.

Nadine studied several of Pierson's latest lectures so if she did meet one of her followers, she could discuss her ideas and theories at length, and if she got stuck, she could simply say Pierson had so many great ideas she couldn't remember them all. She contacted a CC store that sold leather apparel and had them delivered to Room 827. She contacted a CC car rental agency and rented a five-year-old, tan Toyota with Indiana plates that car research showed would blend in with the other cars.

Wearing an ill-fitting frock, she left Room 827 early in the morning with a backpack strapped to her back that contained the leather outfit. She was pleased the desk clerk was in the office and hadn't seen her pass through the lobby. The car was waiting in front of the hotel. She drove to West Lafayette, parked the car on a side street, and walked to the Purdue campus. The first building she came to, she found a restroom where she changed into her leather outfit.

Walking across campus, she observed female students dressed in outfits much like her own which pleased her because there was no need to be concerned about attracting unwanted attention. She went into the student union and found the Oasis Café where she joined other students for their morning cup of coffee.

Pierson's lecture was scheduled to begin at nine and end at eleven. A few minutes before nine, Nadine entered the lecture hall with the other female students to be certain Pierson would be in attendance. Promptly at nine, Pierson mounted the podium dressed in her usual black leather outfit and began speaking.  Content that Pierson was occupied, Nadine left the lecture hall and made her way to Pierson's home.

As she approached the house, she reached into her jacket pocket and pressed the key to deactivate Pierson's alarm system.  She walked up the driveway to a winding flagstone walkway that led to several stone steps that opened onto a landing and the front door.  To her surprise, the door was ajar.  She knocked and in a higher-than-normal Spanish accented voice asked, "*Halo, halo*?"

A nasally Midwestern accent returned, "Yes, I'm here."  A young woman appeared in the hallway and came running to the opened front door.  "I just ran over to check on things for Anita, I mean Ms. Pierson.  She's still pretty nervous about someone trying to hack her computer a while back, sooo..." she paused to emphasize her importance, "she gave me her key to see if everything's in order..." she looked about the house, "and everything is."  She laughed a nervous laugh.

"I wuz yust wid Anita."

"You were?  You lucky bitch.  Isn't she just the greatest?  So radical.  So fucking feminine."

"*Jes*.

"You Spanish?

"*Jes.*"

"You lucky, fuckin' bitch.  Anita loves Spanish chicks." She paused to look more closely at Nadine whose cap visor was pulled low over her forehead partially hiding her face.  "Wow! You *are* one lucky fuckin' bitch.  Anita loves the druggie look. Me?  No luck."  She shrugged her shoulders in dismay.  "Just a plain ole American from Cincinnata, Oh-ho-hum."  She giggled nervously at her Cincinnati and Ohio jokes.  "Anyway, I'm stuck here house- sitting while Anita's lecturing on my favorite subject *Bitch Business*, but…" she drew out the word, "here I am."

"*Qué lástima*.   She asked to me for to get sum *papeles* about…"

"Stop.  I know exactly what she wants.  I'll get them right away."  She ran down the hallway and disappeared.  Moments later she reappeared holding a portfolio stuffed with papers. "I'm sure what she wants is in here."

Nadine reached for the papers, but the young lady was reluctant to hand them over.  "Would you mind, I mean, I know Anita trusts you, you being Spanish, emaciated and all, would you mind if I took this to her myself, and you stay here till she gets back?  I know I'm asking a lot, especially since you're going to miss the best lecture of the semester, but it would mean so much to me if…if, well, you know what I mean."

"*Jes*. I no care. I can stay if *ju* want go."

"You *are* a sweetheart. No wonder Anita trusts you so much. Well, gotta run."

Nadine watched the young woman run down the driveway and into the street. Nadine slipped on a pair of gloves, went to the bedroom, checked the dresser drawers, the bedside table drawers, entered the walk-in closet, and found what she was looking for tucked away on the bottom shelf in an old, red cookie tin: a wad of cash and a bunch of jewelry. She cleaned out the contents of the red cookie tin and left the house careful to leave the door ajar as she had found it and walked down the driveway.

Once on the street, she pressed the key to reactivate the alarm system. She walked calmly onto the Purdue campus, went into one of the building's restrooms, changed out of the leather outfit into the ill-fitting frock, strapped the backpack containing the leather outfit to her back, located the Toyota, and drove back to Chicago.

Nadine breathed a sigh of relief when she entered the hotel lobby because the clerk was busy trying to register a busload of

French Canadians who loudly voiced their anger in a mixture of French and heavily accented English that the accommodations they had paid for did not meet their expectations and most certainly not their satisfaction. She slipped into the elevator and back to her room without anyone having seen her.

# CHAPTER 39

The next morning, Nadine went to the same bank she had visited previously and deposited Pierson's appropriated money into her CC account. The jewelry she put in a safety-deposit-box in the bank's vault. *For safe keeping,* she joked to herself.

She returned to the hotel and to amuse herself scanned the West Lafayette *Journal and Courier's* website for any information pertaining to her appropriation. Nothing. She checked the Purdue campus newspaper, *Exponent,* and found an editorial written by none other than Anita Pierson.

The gist of Pierson's column was a sex pervert, pretending to be a student, had not only violated the sanctity of Pierson's home but had made sexual overtures to one of her students, Mary Edwards, who had not only tried to protect the purity of her own body but the sanctity of Pierson's home. To save herself from unwanted sexual advances, Edwards fled the Pierson home and contacted police, but the thief had already taken the money along with priceless jewelry and fled the scene.

Nadine laughed out loud as she read the article. When she finished, she knew she was born to be an appropriator. It was so much fun appropriating from pompous, arrogant liars.

# CHAPTER 40

Nadine remained at the Cozy Arms Hotel for another two weeks, and during that time, she searched social media for her next associate, and she found him: the President of the Millennial Toffee Company in Seattle: a Jeremy Heagle.

Nadine selected a date for her next appropriation. She contacted CC air-transport that booked her on a corporate jet to Seattle. When she arrived at the Seattle-Tacoma International Airport, a slick-black BMW Sport Coupe awaited her along with a dark blue Ermenegildo Zegna business suit, a white linen blouse, designer hosiery, matching high heels, and an empty briefcase, all carefully placed in the BMW's trunk.

At a hotel near the airport, Nadine changed into the suit and drove to Heagle's home. She parked in front. With briefcase in hand, she casually pressed the key to deactivate the alarms and unlock the front door. One thing she did differently with this appropriation was she programmed an outdated cell phone to chime once when she had been in the associate's residence eight minutes and again at ten minutes. She vowed to leave shortly after the ten-minute warning whether she found funds or not. She never wanted to be inside a residence more than ten minutes.

From her Internet research, she knew the house's layout. She went to the study where she found a safe hidden behind a mirror. Within a minute, she had cracked the safe's combination which was ridiculously easy: Heagle's birthday. Inside were certificates, jewelry, and lots of cash. She opened the briefcase, scooped up the cash and jewelry, closed the safe's door, closed the mirror, exited the house, and pressed the key to reset the alarms.

Once inside the BMW, the cell phone chimed. She had been in the house less than eight minutes. "Yess!" she hissed to herself. She drove to a different hotel, changed out of the suit into casual clothes, and placed the slightly used clothing in the trunk of the BMW. She returned to the airport and parked the BMW in an agreed upon location. Minutes after she parked, she saw a man enter the car and drive it away as she sat aboard a CC corporate jet bound for Miami.

# CHAPTER 41

The following morning Nadine went to a CC bank in Miami and deposited the cash she had appropriated from Heagle in a Swiss bank account as a hedge against a future CC collapse. She then rented a safety-deposit-box where she deposited Heagle's appropriated jewelry: a jewel encrusted Rolex watch, several bejeweled rings, gold chains, several pairs of diamond earrings, and three pearl necklaces.

Upon leaving the bank, she smiled when she looked at her CC bank balance. It was difficult to believe that just the Pierson appropriation alone had already made her fabulously rich. She could live well without any further appropriations for a long time, but *what's the fun in that*? she asked herself. She realized it wasn't just the money that exhilarated her but the selection of the associate, the planning of the appropriation, and its execution that made life exciting: worth living. Without these thrills, life would be nothing.

A few hours later, Nadine checked her cell phone to see if the Heagle appropriation made the news since Heagle was such an important businessman. She watched as her second associate complained bitterly that someone had stolen his most precious possessions: his prized Rolex, diamond rings, gold chains, diamond earrings that had been in the family for years, and pearl necklaces that had belonged to his recently departed great grandmother. One reporter shouted out, "How much was it all worth?"

"More than a million," Heagle angrily retorted.

*Nice haul, Nadine,* she murmured to herself.

Pleased with the results of her second appropriation, she set about her next bit of business. She contacted CC's forged document's department and applied for visas and passports to travel abroad. She was pleased to learn all the required documents would be ready in two days. In high spirits, she danced about the hotel suite and in an affected British accent said, "The summer season is upon us, Nigel. Don't you think it would be positively divine to spend the season on the Riviera?' and in her best Nigel voice answered, "But of course, my darling. What a positively smashing idea." Nadine contacted CC's French Riviera home rentals and within minutes booked a beautiful villa overlooking the Mediterranean for the entire high season. *Now that's what I'm talkin' 'bout,"* she uttered to herself.

# CHAPTER 42

The chauffeur-driven Bentley followed the long winding road to its end where resided a luxurious one-story glass house whose walls protruded well beyond the edge of a perilous cliff that rose high above the blue waters of the Mediterranean. The large expanses of glass reflected the bright afternoon sun. It was an impressive sight not lost on Nadine.

A short, unattractive man awaited her arrival belying Nadine's concept that all Frenchmen were tall and good looking. He waited until the chauffeur opened the rear door of the Bentley before introducing himself as Blanchard Bleu from the realty company. He spoke French, and when Nadine didn't ask him to speak English, he opened the front door of the house and continued in French. He showed her the house's amenities including the beach far below the cantilevered house. "The house is magnificent, no, *Mademoiselle?* How far it hangs over the edge of the cliff, and more than 40 meters below this magnificent house is the beach. Of course, it is private. No one of the public can come here.  Only members of the community such as yourself.  There are so few houses along this stretch of beach.  You should be alone if you so desire, but a pretty young lady such as yourself I'm sure will want many guests."  He flashed a leering smile.  Nadine looked away.

"Of course, you will want to be careful going down to the beach.  The path is steep.  That is why the owner of the property has instructed me to caution you and to ask you to use the rope attached to the poles to go down and to help you come back up.  That feature is very important.  I understand you are having all your meals delivered?" he asked, changing the subject.

"*Oui,* Nadine answered.

He handed Nadine a remote.  "This will open both the front door and the door to the beach path.  I don't know all the other things it can do.  I leave it for you to see what happens.  Nothing bad, that much I can assure you.  If there are no further questions, I wish you a most happy stay.  Are there any questions?

"*Non,* Nadine answered.

"In that case, *adieu.*"

Alone, Nadine surveyed her beautiful surroundings through the massive glass windows that showcased the calm, blue waters of the Mediterranean and the crystal, clear sky above.

# CHAPTER 43

Because the weather took a turn for the worse, Nadine spent the next few days getting used to her new surroundings: namely the fact she was suspended in mid-air over the edge of a gigantic cliff. For the first day, she was afraid to move for fear the house might collapse onto the beach below, but by the second day, she realized the house wasn't going to fall off the cliff, so she relaxed: a bit.

Nadine found the bedroom the most comfortable and coziest room in the house with its wraparound drapes that, when drawn, darkened the room and gave a pleasant sense of security. She enjoyed playing with the remote opening and closing the drapes in the bedroom and the shades that covered the huge windows overlooking the Mediterranean, turning on and off the many television sets in the various rooms, logging onto the Internet, and scanning a music service with hundreds of channels.  As the days passed, she felt more and more at home in her new home.

With the return of good weather, the allure of the white sandy beach mixed with a tinge of red captivated Nadine.  She decided it was time to investigate: especially the redness of the sand: something she hadn't noticed previously.  Wearing a string bikini and carrying a beach-bag that contained a large towel, suntan oil, and a bottle of cold water, she slowly descended the steep path.  No one had to tell her to hold on to the rope.  The steepness of the twisty, narrow, sandy path demanded she hold onto it if she wanted to stay alive.

Once on the beach, she turned to look up at the house that extended well beyond the cliff's edge.  *Incredible,* she thought to herself.  She lay down on the beach towel to get a closer look at the reddish tinged sand.  She wondered where it came from.  She made a mental note to search the Internet for the answer, but that could wait until later.  For the moment, she wanted one thing: to soak up the warm Mediterranean sun.  Lying in the sun's radiant rays, she fought to erase all thoughts of her confinement in the hole, but that was impossible.  She realized she was scarred for life.

# CHAPTER 44

Weeks passed, and Blanchard Bleu, the little man from the real estate agency, had been right. It seemed as if the sandy beach and the blue waters of the Mediterranean were reserved for Nadine's personal use. She hadn't seen a single person since her arrival, and she didn't expect to because even on a clear day not a single house was visible.

Over the weeks, she established a routine. In the late afternoon, when the sun was less intense, she went down to the beach for a refreshing swim and to lie on the sand and let it sift slowly through her fingers. The mystery of the red sand had been solved long ago. The storms when she first arrived had blown reddish colored sand from the Sahara and deposited it on the Riviera's beaches, but the red color, much to Nadine's disappointment, had nearly disappeared blown away to some other distant place.

During these few weeks, as she lay alone on the beach letting the soft sands of the Mediterranean sift between her fingers, the sandy solitude gave her the opportunity to analyze herself and discover who she was. She liked the fact she was independent: that she didn't need other people. She prided herself on her self-reliance: that she was able to take care of herself without her parents or anyone else's help, although she had to admit she owed some of her success to CC. The thought of those two letters, CC, brought back memories of her captivity and the hole, but even through those grim days when faced with starvation, thirst, and the fear of dying in that dark dungeon, she had maintained her strength and most important: her sanity. She had not only survived. She had triumphed. She liked these things about herself.

She also liked the fact she had the foresight to plan for the future especially at the early age of ten and every year thereafter researching the Internet for all the skills she would need to become an appropriator. But her *pièce de résistance* was the discovery of the CC Bank with its spectacularly high rate of interest that made her a fabulously rich woman in a matter of months.

There was one more attribute she greatly prized: her intelligence. This gave her the self-confidence not only to take control of her own life but to control and manipulate the lives of others.  She first realized she was a control-freak when she discovered the sexual gratification of control and manipulation prom night.  She remembered the elation and the wicked pleasure that she, and she alone, had not only controlled the evenings events but had manipulated her teachers and classmates into believing she was someone she wasn't.  *That's power,* she sneered to herself as she reflected on those precious moments.  *Better than sex any time.*

She realized this desire to control people was another reason why she wanted to appropriate her associates' money and jewelry because she appropriated more than their wealth.  She appropriated their trust: their self-confidence.  She made them afraid.  She controlled them.  She liked that.

Something she hadn't come to grips with was her beauty and its sexual complications. After considerable thought, she decided not to hide her attractiveness but to enhance it and use it as a weapon as she had prom night.  She reveled in the knowledge she was cruel: that she loved to inflict emotional suffering on others.

As she lay on the beach watching the wavelets come and go, she concluded she was a greedy, self-centered bitch who cared about no one but herself.  *I'm not a very nice person,* she thought to herself, *but that's who I am.*

# CHAPTER 45

adine had never done it, but she had read about it on social media and seen it enough times on YouTube to make her want to try it: nude sunbathing: on the French Riviera. *I'm here,* she reasoned. *Why not?* After more than a month of swimming and sunbathing, she hadn't seen a single, solitary soul. She removed the skimpy bikini and lay back on the beach towel to enjoy the late afternoon sun *au natural.* Much to her surprise, nudity brought new unexpected pleasures of freedom and a sexual pride in her body. For the first time in her life, she took pleasure in her breasts. She became aware of her body as an outward expression of her inner self. She laughed at the thought that her body was the perfect Venus Flytrap to trap men's emotions and twist them to her will.

Another month passed. Her reward for the daily trips to the beach was a sun-bronzed body that glistened in the sun. One afternoon, just as she prepared to leave the beach, she heard faint sounds of music in the distance. *There goes the neighborhood,* she thought to herself.

Days passed. She continued her daily ritual of sunbathing in the late afternoon but no longer *au natural.* She wore a skimpy bikini as protection against prying eyes. One afternoon after her swim, she lay on the beach towel lost in thought when she heard a male voice say in French, "Good afternoon, pretty lady."

She looked up to see three male bodies hunched over staring down at her and said, "This is a private beach. Please leave."

Undeterred by Nadine's brusqueness, the three young men stood to their full height, each displaying his wares to the fullest extent their tight Speedos would allow. Unimpressed, Nadine told them to leave her private beach immediately whereupon one of them said, "Don't you want to meet your neighbors?"

"Not interested."

"We introduce ourselves anyway. I'm Esme. The others are Ives and Ruben. Don't bother with them. I'm the handsomest."

"Perhaps so," Nadine answered, "but he," pointing to Ruben, "has more to offer."

Ives and Ruben burst into laughter slapping each other on the back and jabbing at Esme's ribs. "I see the pretty lady has eyes. She knows what she likes," Ruben boasted to the others.

"And what I like is peace and quiet. Three's a crowd. I go now." She picked up her beach towel and climbed the trail to the house while the three young men stood admiring every step she took.

# CHAPTER 46

Nadine realized the game she was about to play was risky, but *that's the purpose of the exercise,* she mused to herself. She was curious if the young men on the beach had understood her *three's crowd* comment. She would have to wait and see if it registered in their Gallic brains.

The next day she sat by the window with a clear view of the beach below while she scanned the Internet for her next associate. Her summer lease was about to expire which meant she had to plan her next move. With winter just a few short months away, she had to decide if she wanted to stay in a warm southern climate or brave the cold winter winds of the north where the wealthier associates resided.

Late in the morning, she saw one of the young men staring up at the house. It appeared he was trying to make up his mind whether to climb the steep path to the house or stay on the beach.  After several minutes of indecision, he jogged back down the beach.

The early afternoon brought another one of the young men who like the previous one stood staring up at the house hoping to catch a glimpse of the pretty lady.  She could tell it was a different young man because he was wearing a magenta shirt while the first one wore a light blue shirt.  *How thoughtful of them to color code themselves,* she laughed to herself.  She speculated what the third one might wear.  *Maybe nothing,* she joked.  Nevertheless, she guessed he would wear a dark green shirt, the least expected color she could think of.  She even picked the time he would arrive: 4:12. One thing she did know: she wouldn't be on the beach.  She would let their anxiety build before she released it.

The 4:12 hour arrived and so did the third young man dressed in of all things a dark green shirt.  Nadine roared with laughter at the sight.  He did the same as the others.  He stared at the house hoping for a glimpse of the pretty lady.  When he didn't see her, he turned and jogged down the beach.  *At least they got my threesome message,* she thought to herself.

# CHAPTER 47

Nadine didn't go to the beach for several days. As the days passed, each of the young men jogged alone up the beach, saw she wasn't there, kicked at the sand in disappointment, and went back down the beach. As the sun set on the fourth day, it seemed as if the three young men had given up the pursuit. None of them appeared.

On the morning of the fifth day, one of the young men jogged alone along the water's edge, stopped, and stared at the glass enclosed house perched on the cliff. Nadine knew this was the moment to strike. She had separated him from the others. *He's the winner,* she joked to herself.

She slipped out of her shorts and blouse into the skimpy bikini, picked up a bag that contained suntan oil, several bottles of water, a towel large enough for two, clicked the remote to open the beach door, and started down the tortuous path. She noticed the young man had started back down the beach kicking at the sand with each step in bitter disappointment.

Halfway down the path, she saw him turn back for one last, hopeful look.  Even at a considerable distance, she could see disappointment turn to excitement and joy as his whole body came to life at the sight of her.  He waved his arms, jumped up and down like a little boy, and quickly ran toward the path that led down from the house.  She slowly descended the path making certain to appear as if she would fall at the very next step.  None of this was wasted on the young man who rushed up the path to give his male support fearing she might be hurt or even killed when he saw her struggle with the treacherous path. Together they descended the path to the sandy beach.

Neither said a word. They didn't need to. He was honored to be in her presence, to help her in any way he could, and she reveled in how easy it was to control him.  She was gratified that such a fine male specimen as Ives had no effect on her.  What she was about to do she considered nothing more than a way to test her sexual skills.

When they were safely on the beach, she looked at him and smiled a devastating smile.  She saw the effect the single smile had on him.  She knew she had stolen his heart.  He was hers, but she intended to steal more than just his heart. She wanted his soul: something that would bind him to her for the rest of his life.

She unzipped the beach bag and took out the towel and spread it on the sand. She lay on one-side making it obvious she wanted him to lie next to her. Ives brushed the sand from his feet before lying on the beach towel. He wanted to satisfy her in every way he could even with as simple an act as brushing sand from his feet so as not to defile her realm.

None of this was wasted on Nadine. She realized he had experienced love at first sight: something she never believed in until that moment. She laughed to herself that if she wasn't such a bitch, he most certainly would have stolen her heart.

They lay quietly on the towel watching the soft white clouds drift aimlessly across the azure sky. How much time passed neither had any idea, but time wasn't important. Ives savored every moment. He drank her in as if she were a fine wine. He was content just to lie next to her. For her, she wanted to tease him as much as she could hoping he would cum in his Speedos without her having to do much more than expose her breasts and private part.

She gently took his right hand in hers and after a few moments of handholding, she raised his hand to the delicate fibers that covered her breasts. She felt his body jerk when his hand touched the fabric and heard him gasp at the unexpected pleasure. She raised up on her arms and glanced down at his Speedo. It had expanded with this one gesture. Nadine smiled to herself that all was going according to plan.

She lay back down, unfastened the bikini straps, and guided his hand beneath the fabric. She could feel his hand tremble. From the expression on his face, touching her breast was a deep emotional experience for him.

She rolled on top of him and pressed her lips gently against his cheek. He put his arms around her. She could feel his long, warm fingers lovingly caress her back. She placed her lips over his and felt them greedily embrace hers.

She rolled onto her back exposing her bronzed breasts that glistened in the sun. He lay on his side and looked at them for some time before he dared touch them. She started to free the bottom of her bikini when he spoke. "No. Don't. I want more than to possess your body. I want you to love me as I love you. I know this is not true for you: yet. I hope in time you will come to love me. I will wait."

Nadine realized he was after the same things she was: mind and soul. The difference between them was he wanted her love, her trust, her loyalty, her sexual being while she wanted to control and dominate him for her own aggrandizement and selfish means.

"May I come back tomorrow?" he whispered.

Nadine nodded her head *yes*. He stood. His erect penis filled his Speedo. He saw her look at it. He smiled. "I will take care of him when I get home." He turned and jogged down the beach.

# CHAPTER 48

The morning sun rose high in the sky promising another beautiful day. Nadine sat by the huge window watching for Ives. She was certain he would appear sometime during the morning hours as he had the previous day. When he hadn't appeared by noon, she decided he either had problems getting rid of Esme and Ruben or had lost interest. She shrugged her shoulders in a care-free manner and thought: *who knows? Who cares?*

About one o'clock, one of the young men appeared. She couldn't be certain who it was until he blew kisses at the huge windows above. She knew it was Ives. She quickly changed out of her shorts and blouse into a skimpy bikini. She took one last glance out the window before she grabbed her beach bag. Ives was no longer alone. Two others had joined him.

She sat in a chair waiting for them to leave when she saw Ives suddenly push the other two. They pushed back. One of them punched Ives.  He punched back, but punches from the other two sent him sprawling.  He threw fists-full of sand in the faces of the other two.  In a blind rage, they kicked his legs repeatedly and beat him about the chest and face with their fists.

Two of the young men left.  The third lay in the sand for some time before he summoned the strength to stand.  He stood, swaying like a tree in a windstorm.  He looked up at the house on the cliff.  He turned and limped slowly down the beach.

The fight lasted only a minute, but even from a distance, Nadine could see irreparable damage had been done to the young men's friendship.  *The mysteries of men,* she thought to herself. *Years of friendship destroyed in seconds by a girl whose name they never knew.* She lowered the shades over the huge glass windows. She never opened them again.  She had seen enough of the white sandy beach and the blue waters of the Mediterranean.  As for the young men, she never saw them again.

# CHAPTER 49

Nadine boarded a plane for Madrid the next morning. She had had enough sexual adventures. She wanted to return to a normal life which meant appropriating an associate's wealth. There was one problem: her rule of only one appropriation per year: a rule she designed so as not to arouse unnecessary police suspicion and to preserve her freedom. She knew she had to heed it or face the consequences, and she had had enough of those.

In Madrid, she checked into a five-star CC hotel. It was here she rethought her career as an appropriator. It was no secret to Nadine she enjoyed hurting people emotionally. Pierson's-Heagle's sanctimonious whining, however, revealed another dimension she never considered: that the arrogant rich seemingly impervious to the suffering of others could be emotionally hurt if relieved of their most precious possessions. She decided to focus future appropriations on the world's most powerful, influential individuals whose precious possessions she would keep locked up in safety-deposit-boxes in CC bank vaults where they would be safe and never seen again.

# CHAPTER 50

Bud Perkins, affectionately called Perky by his colleagues, was *a damned good agent* according to everyone who worked with him at the FBI. This well-earned accolade was due to his meticulous investigative procedures and his tenacity because he never stopped working a case until it was solved. During his years with the bureau, he had arrested or assisted in the arrest of numerous hard-core criminals.

One afternoon, Perky was in his office working his way through a mound of paperwork when he heard a soft knock on the opened door. He stood when he saw the FBI Director, James Uhler, enter his office. After the usual pleasantries were exchanged, Uhler asked what he was currently working on. "The usual: drugs, gangs, and terrorists," Perky replied.

"How about a little change of pace?" When Uhler saw a quizzical look cross Perky's face, he added, "I can't free you from the usual, but in your spare time, if you ever have any, I want you to work the Estate Case." He handed Perky a portfolio. "Look this over when you have time. That's all I ask."

Perky frowned. "I can't promise you much. The opioid crisis is taking most of my time these days. If I ever get a handle on that, I'll give EC a look-see."

"I understand. Just do the best you can, whenever you can," Uhler said casually over his shoulder as he left Perky's office.

Perky was not unfamiliar with the Estate Case, so-called because it dealt with just the most affluent, most powerful people in society. Police departments both domestic and foreign had worked the case for years without success so they turned to Interpol, the FBI, and the CIA for help. It wasn't the number of robberies that concerned them: just one a year. It was who had been robbed: heads of state, CEOs of Fortune 500 Companies, famous showbusiness personalities, and highly respected members of the clergy. What further complicated the case was those who had been robbed didn't want to co-operate with law enforcement agencies who wanted access to their internet files, cell phone conversations, and an accurate description of the items that had been stolen as well as their worth. Many unconfirmed sources guessed the total take from the robberies could be in excess of fifty million dollars while others thought no more than ten.  Whatever the number, significant amounts of money and jewelry had been stolen from individuals who might have *borrowed* certain items from others, hence their skittishness at helping law enforcement reclaim their losses. *The plot thickens,* Perky thought to himself as he placed the EC folder in the bottom- left-hand-drawer of his desk.

# CHAPTER 51

Two years passed since Perky had put the EC folder in the bottom-left-hand-drawer of his desk. Although he hadn't looked at it since the day Uhler left his office, he had spent hours thinking about it. Two puzzling aspects of the case held intense interest for him. How did the suspect get past the most sophisticated security systems in the world, and why did exterior and interior security cameras freeze, locked doors unlock, but the time stamps continued to function?

Another interesting facet of the case was the single chime that sounded at eight-and ten-minute intervals. This one fact most definitely linked all EC robberies together: a fact Perky hoped would be the downfall of the suspect. If he could trace that chime to a particular timer or watch, he might have a break in the case. He was also interested if the suspect knew the mechanism used to freeze the cameras didn't silence the sound. Perky pondered this point for some time unable to come to any conclusion.

He decided to work on the chime thing to see if he could link it to any particular device.  After many days of intense research, he found the chime on a cell phone no longer in production which gave a clue that the perpetrator was either an older person who didn't want to upgrade to a newer cell phone or a younger person who didn't have the money.  He ruled out the young person theory because of the sophisticated electro-engineering needed to freeze the cams.  He was certain the suspect had to be an older man who was an electro-magnetic engineer with nerves of steel to steal from the influential rich.

For the next year, Perky chased this lead unable to isolate a single electro-engineer capable of such an engineering feat who was in any of the locations on the days the robberies had occurred.  *Damn,* Perky muttered under his breath.  *Another lead gone sour.*  Then it happened.  Terrorist attacks occurred in four major cities: three in Europe and one in the US with hundreds dead and thousands more injured.  These tragedies forced him to stop work on the EC case and focus on finding the suspects behind the attacks.

# CHAPTER 52

**E**ven though Perky devoted his efforts to finding those responsible for the terrorist attacks, he noticed robberies of the rich and famous continued at the rate of one per year. He kept careful records of these events so he could refer to them at a later date that was over three years in coming. It came with the arrest of Neo-Nazis who, masquerading as Moslem terrorists, set bombs at strategic chock points in malls, train stations, and airports so each explosion would kill or maim as many innocent people as possible. The arrests shocked the civilized world that Nazis had the power to execute a multi-national plan with such devastating results. The robbery of the world's richest woman, Theodora Friedenberg, an award-winning Dutch novelist, movie director, and chairwoman of the EU's financial board, garnered nary a headline as the Nazi bombings dominated the news.

With the Nazi terrorists in custody, Perky reacquainted himself with the EC case. It was when he played the tape of the Friedenberg robbery that he heard a new tone at the eight and ten-minute marks. He searched for the tone and found it within an hour. It was the default tone for the new Giga-Phone 3 that had been on sale for less than a week. He rushed to his superior to inform him of his find. Within minutes, agents throughout the world went to stores that sold the Giga-Phone 3 while others subpoenaed the company's sales records looking for an older man whose past and present buying habits might suggest an ability to manipulate electric currents to freeze cameras and unlock locked doors.

By Giga-Phone standards the sale of several hundred thousand phones was a weak introduction of their new product, but for Perky and the worldwide network of agents, it was a huge number. Even with narrowing the number down to men forty and over, the number of suspects exceeded 100,000, yet Perky was convinced this was the breakthrough he was looking for. He was determined to follow this lead to its conclusion.

# CHAPTER 53

Six years passed.  Perky worked the EC case as much as he could during those years, but other cases kept interrupting his investigation.  Whenever time permitted, he sifted through Giga-Phone 3 customer data still convinced a man forty or older was the EC suspect. Nevertheless, he feared his list of Giga-Phone 3 buyers had gone stale with the passage of so much time: time that was on the side of the criminal because he was no closer to solving the case than he had been when he first started.

Late one night, his tired eyes happened to fall on the name of a Chicago locksmith who at the time of his arrest was in his early fifties.  No follow up had been done other than the man's arrest record because Perky had identified the EC suspect as an electro-magnetic engineer.  No one had ever considered a locksmith as a possible suspect.

Perky decided to pursue this quasi lead: namely because he didn't have any others.  He contacted the Chicago police in hopes they might be able to shed some light on who the man was and why he was arrested.  The Chicago police were slow to respond.  Weeks passed with no answer.  Perky was on his third cup of coffee one rainy morning when a terse message from the Chicago police came through: *Luther Wilson Records Sealed.*

*Records Sealed* raised Perky's antenna that perhaps he was on to something.  He immediately contacted his colleague, Matt Licata, who was less than interested.  "The last time you got one of your ideas, it cost this department and other departments around the world millions of dollars, euros, yen, and whatever else."

"All I'm asking is a court order to open the file."

"The arrest of a locksmith isn't a high priority in any police department.  Besides, the files have probably been destroyed by now.  I'm sorry to say this to you, but this is just another of your wild goose chases."

"Perhaps yes: perhaps no. What's the harm in asking the court to unseal a twenty- plus-year-old file?  If it's been destroyed: dead-end.  If it exists, we have a quick look-see.  If there's anything we can use, we use it.   All we have to do is prove," he air-quoted with his fingers the word *prove*, "that it's a question of national security we unseal this file.  Simple as that."

"Simple as that," Licata mocked Perky.  "You know the court's going to ask what proof we have unsealing the file is in the interest of national security.  There's a big difference between thinking, knowing, and being able to prove," he air-quoted the word *prove*, "the necessity of the unsealing which, for your information, is my job not yours."

"That's why they pay you the big bucks."  Perky smiled a sarcastic smile.

# CHAPTER 54

"Christ, Perky," Licata barked as he stormed into Perky's office slamming the door behind him. "You've kicked in a goddamned hornet's nest." He paused to collect himself as he smoothed back his hair. "The good news is the Wilson files exist. You'll never guess where they are?"

"In some dark basement?"

"Close. They're in Washington: in: of all places: the National Archives."

"You gotta be shittin' me."

"After I explained the strong possibility that by releasing the Wilson files the FBI might be able to solve the EC case, the court demanded the files be opened *post haste*. Guess whose files they are?"

"No idea."

"Ours. The FBI's. However." Licata paused as he looked Perky in the eye. "There's a problem. Our fearless leader, James Uhler, refuses to release the files even at the court's request. More than likely he hid them in the most unlikely place, the Archives, hoping to bury them." He held up his hand to silence Perky. "It gets even better. During the court proceedings, unbeknownst to the general public, one of the judges, Alice Morrison, was deprived of her money and jewels. She's mad as hell. Naturally she wants her property back without notoriety. *Ergo*, she and the other justices have demanded Uhler unseal the Chicago locksmith's file. Now we'll find out all the shit Uhler's been hiding all these years."

# CHAPTER 55

After much wrangling, Director Uhler finally released the Wilson files with restrictions. Only Perkins could access the files for no more than eight hours. Perkins couldn't take any notes or photographs of the materials contained therein. As soon as Perkins completed his inquiry, the lock shop files were to be sealed and remain sealed for the duration. Upon exiting the Archives, Perkins was to report his findings and conclusions directly to Director Uhler and no one else. The court acceded to these demands.

Perky was led to a secured room deep in the bowels of the National Archives where he began his analysis of the locksmith files. He discovered the Chicago Police Department had the locksmith's shop under surveillance for more than a year. They suspected Luther Wilson, the lock shop's owner, of being the kingpin of a world-wide narcotics network. Once the Chicago P.D. arrested Wilson, the FBI swooped down and relieved them of their catch.  Uhler and the FBI took full credit for the arrest of the drug kingpin while the Chicago P.D. nursed its wounded pride and counted up the many dollars and cents it spent on surveillance.

Perky decided to watch the tapes the Chicago P.D. had taken over the course of the investigation.  Surprisingly, the shop had few visitors but the ones who did enter were a suspicious looking lot except for a young, white girl with frizzy hair.  She entered the shop but was inside for less than thirty seconds before she left.  Out of all the people who entered the shop, she was the only one who didn't fit the surroundings: young white girl in a black neighborhood: in a lock shop owned by a middle-aged black locksmith.  What did they have in common?  Was it drugs, was she lost, or was it something else?

# CHAPTER 56

As Perky sat in the basement of the National Archives, he continued to ponder why a young, frizzy-haired girl would be in a black neighborhood and enter a seedy-looking shop. It wasn't until he watched the tape numerous times he realized Wilson put something in the girl's left hand. What could a black locksmith put in the hand of a young, white girl? Drugs? Unlikely. The girl could have gotten those any number of places without the risk of entering an unfriendly neighborhood. No. She didn't go into the shop to get drugs, but that theory led back to why was she in the locksmith's shop.

Suddenly it hit him. The young, white girl wasn't lost. She knew exactly where she was going and what she wanted. A key, but why would she want a key from Wilson?

Perky stared into space as he began to put the pieces together. He theorized that Wilson was not an ordinary locksmith, but the ingenious inventor of a key that could freeze cams and unlock locked doors. "Holy shit!" he yelled out loud as he slapped his forehead with the palm of his hand.

Hands shaking with excitement, he knocked on the door of the secured room. An unsmiling armed guard opened the door and searched him to be certain he wasn't trying to smuggle any documents out of the Archives. He informed Perky he still had over an hour left to review the documents in question. Perky thanked him as he scurried out of the room to catch the first plane to New York.

The plane landed in New York at 7:39 p.m. Once inside the terminal, Perky called Licata on Licata's private cell. When Licata answered, Perky whispered into the phone, "It's me, Perky."

"Yeah. I see that. You know I'm not supposed to talk to you until after you clear everything with Uhler."

"We need to meet. Meet me at the Ascot Diner on Astoria as soon as you can. I'll be there. It's important. Trust me."

# CHAPTER 57

An hour later, Licata walked into the Ascot Diner. He saw Perky sitting in a booth. He slipped into the booth opposite him. "Talk," was all he whispered.

Perky leaned forward over the table. He looked to his left to be certain no one was nearby. In a subdued voice, he said, "You've got to go back to the courts. You've got to convince them that lyin', son-of-a-bitch Uhler only gave me half of the Wilson file. He left out the best parts: the proof I need to convict a whole bunch of people," he paused for effect, "including him." Perky saw fear in Licata's eyes.

"Christ, Perky, I'm already in a pile of shit just talking to you. Did you forget you were supposed to report to Uhler directly and no one else? Must I remind you as of this moment we could both lose our jobs, our pensions not to mention our freedom? I'm bailing." He stood to leave.

Perky grabbed his arm. "You selfish bastard! Our job is to catch the bad guys not cover our own asses."

"Maybe I am a selfish bastard, but I've got a wife and three kids to support. Who have you got? Nobody but your own self."

"Okay. Leave, but if you do, I'll resign from the bureau, and it won't be a silent resignation. I'll drag you, Uhler, the bureau, and everyone else connected with this case through the fuckin' mud. As I see it, Licata, you're in a lose-lose situation. Do you wanna go down sitting on your lazy ass or do your job and catch the guilty bastards?"

"Jesus, Perky," was all Licata said as he sat back down.

# CHAPTER 58

Licata did as Perky asked. He petitioned the court to reopen the Chicago Locksmith Case now referred to as the Wilson Case. The court denied Licata's request based on Uhler's fervent denials he had not withheld evidence and was dismayed the court would ever entertain the notion he would act in such an unprofessional manner. After two years passed and two additional robberies that involved the Canadian Prime Minister and a famous Hollywood actress, the court, through back channels, requested Licata to re-petition his request for additional information on the Wilson Case now that Uhler was no longer Director of the FBI.

A totally different person, Samantha Krull, a no-nonsense, former persecutor whose deepest desire was to lock up the bad girls and boys was appointed FBI Director. The Wilson Case with possible implications to the Estate Case greatly interested her.

Once the court approved the renewing of the investigation, Krull directed agents to search the database for the more than twenty-some-year-old files on Luther Wilson. After considerable digging, the agents hit pay dirt. Files labeled *Luther Wilson: Classified* were located and declassified. Krull assigned the case to her best agent who was the first to bring the case to her attention: Perky.

# CHAPTER 59

One thing that bothered Perky was why had Uhler come to his office years ago and offered him the EC files? The only thing he could think of was Uhler was feeling heat from those who had been robbed to solve the case and get back their stolen stuff with no questions asked. Uhler had given him just enough information in hopes he might be able to solve the case without implicating him, the bureau, or any other corrupt individuals.

Now that Director Krull had given him *carte blanche* to take as much time as he needed to sift through not just the WC files but any other files relevant to the case, the Luther Wilson case quickly unraveled. Wilson was a drug kingpin. No surprise there. One question that bugged Perky was why had Wilson bought a Giga-Phone 3 if he was supposed to be in prison on narcotic charges that should have gotten him a life sentence without parole? The answer was simple. Uhler cut a deal offering him immunity.  Perky wondered what information Wilson could possibly have that would tempt Uhler to give him immunity.

The answer came hidden deep in the files.  Luther Wilson was more than just a drug dealer. He was also a wheeler-dealer in a mysterious virtual currency called Crypto-Coin that offered huge returns on money invested.  It was through Crypto-Coin Wilson laundered millions of his drug dollars converting those millions into billions.  In exchange for immunity, Wilson exposed the entire CC operation to the FBI.  That explained the near collapse of CC more than twenty-years ago.

Perky asked himself the following question.  If Uhler had made public Wilson's arrest, what would have happened differently?  Luther Wilson most certainly would have been a dead man, and CC would have changed its protocols before the FBI could have launched any attack against it enabling vicious criminals to continue their operations.  Perky realized Uhler had done the right thing as distasteful as it was to give Wilson immunity.

These facts changed Perky's mind.  Instead of Uhler being the lyin' son-of-a-bitch he supposed him to be, he respected Uhler's decision.  Now he faced the same dilemma as Uhler had. Should he release all he knew about Wilson and Uhler to the public or should he keep it secret?  Perky knew the answer as had Uhler.  Some things best remain secret.

# CHAPTER 60

Perky contacted the Chicago Police Department asking for more information about the Luther Wilson lockshop case focusing not on Wilson but the young, white girl. He inquired if there was any additional tape of the girl or if anyone still on the force had been a part of the surveillance team who could shed more light on the case.

With Director Krull's permission, he sent emails to every high school in the country asking them to review yearbooks for the years he specified for female students with what he described as having frizzy hair and to send these photos along with student names and addresses as well as the school's name and address to his FBI email addresses. Within days, Perky had to ask for additional secretarial help to process the thousands of yearbook pictures that poured in.

Agents then contacted parents: a laborious task because after more than twenty years, many parents had moved or passed away. Old landline, cell phone numbers, email addresses had been changed or discontinued further complicating the investigation. Nevertheless, agents fanned out across the country ringing doorbells of parents and neighbors to confirm whether the girl in question had been seen or heard from within the last year. Once a girl's status had been positively confirmed, her name was stricken from a list of over 70,000 names that continued to grow each day instead of shrink.

# CHAPTER 61

**M**any months later Perky received an email from the Chicago Police Department with a note: *All personnel who worked on the Luther Wilson case have either passed or are in ill health. However, I found the additional tape you requested. The last few seconds were omitted from the investigation since the individual in question was a minor and had committed no crime. Hope the included tape will be of use. Sgt. William Clark, Property Clerk, Chicago Police Department.*

Perky immediately handed the tape over to the bureau's photo recognition department that analyzed the few seconds of tape seeking to establish facial recognition. It was a pains-taking task because of the out-of-date black and white equipment used by the Chicago P.D. plus years of storage that had further degraded the tape. After careful analysis, agents found one grainy frame suitable for facial recognition. Once that had been established, they scanned the high school yearbook pictures that had been sent to the bureau.

One early afternoon, Perky's phone rang. It was Eleanor from photo recognition. She skipped the usual pleasantries knowing Perky was a man who appreciated directness and said, "I got your girl, Perky. Name is Nadine Car."

Perky was speechless. After a few moments, Eleanor laughingly asked, "Cat got your tongue?"

Finally finding his voice, he whispered, "Yeah. I've been chasing this cat for years. Thanks, Eleanor."

# CHAPTER 62

erky had to make the most important decision of his life: one that would jeopardize not just his FBI career but his personal life. If he didn't inform domestic and foreign law agencies Car's name, physical description, personal information, and facial recognition data, he faced dismissal from the bureau and arrest for withholding pertinent information.

No one in the bureau knew he had resumed work on the EC case which allowed him to make the decision his way and not the bureau's. He ruled out informing Interpol and foreign law agencies. He didn't trust any of them to maintain the information's integrity. Besides, he knew his suspect was an American. He reasoned the woman in question would sooner or later appear in one of this country's security cameras. However, he needed to restrict the number of people who would have access to the facial recognition data. He sent it to American airport security agencies with specific instructions that the person who matched the profile was to be detained, cell phone confiscated, and the individual was to remain in police custody until he, Bud Perkins, arrived at the scene.

# CHAPTER 63

Nadine's flight was grounded because of bad weather. After a four-hour delay, conditions improved sufficiently for the flight to continue. It landed in Chicago about two p.m. The next flight to Kansas City wasn't for another five hours. As if that wasn't bad enough, first class on the Kansas City flight had been sold out with no cancellations. The only seat available was in coach.

Such inconveniences justified Nadine's intense hatred of all commercial airlines. She hated being subjected to the dehumanizing aspects of having to share the same space with so many strange strangers, and she particularly hated the long concourses commercial airlines forced its passengers to traverse. She much preferred to fly on a corporate jet that once it landed coasted into a heated hangar where she could disembark the plane in privacy, but due to the weather, none was available.

As she walked down the long concourse at the Kansas City International Airport with her black luggage carrier trailing behind her, she felt vulnerable. She attributed this to the long delays, cramped coach seating, and the fact she was tired and hungry.

As she neared the end of the concourse, she saw two men dressed in dark suits. She passed them thinking they were waiting for another passenger. Once she entered the terminal, she turned and saw the two men she had passed walking behind her. She faced forward and saw two men leave a shop and walk toward her. They stopped ahead of her. One of the men said, "Hand me your shoulder bag, please. Your cell phone inside?"

Nadine nodded her head *yes*.

"Follow me, please," the man commanded.

Nadine realized her career as an appropriator had come to an end.

# CHAPTER 64

Nadine expected to be hustled into an airport backroom or taken to a Kansas City jail to be interrogated. Instead, she was escorted through the terminal and out the main entrance to a waiting black, windows-darkened SUV. As the SUV wended its way through traffic, she wasn't certain if she was being abducted by CC, the Kansas City Police, or the FBI. This was a moment she hoped would never come. She thought she had prepared herself in the event it did, but the fear of being locked in a hole with no hope of ever leaving it alive was too strong.

Much to her relief, the SUV pulled up in front of a five-star hotel. She was led through the lobby to a bank of elevators one of which opened as she and the four men approached. One of the men pushed the 33rd floor button. When the doors opened, the men guided her to a suite that was more luxurious than the one CC had provided years ago.

One of the men finally spoke. He asked if she was hungry. When she said *yes,* he notified room service to bring up sandwiches, coffee, fresh fruit, and cookies: enough for five. He pointed to an opened door that led into a bedroom. Nadine was amazed at the spaciousness of the bedroom and the bathroom with its marble walls, floor, and ceiling with gold fixtures in the double sink and shower. Such luxury she hadn't expected.

"I suggest you make yourself comfortable," the man said. "I'll notify you when the food comes."

She took a shower and changed into her night gown. A light knock on the door signaled the food had arrived. She opened the door and found the man on the other side holding a tray. She took the tray, thanked him, and closed the door behind her.

As she ate a sandwich, she pondered why she was in such a luxurious suite and not some dingy jail cell. She didn't know who had detained her or why, but she suspected something big was in the offering. What big meant, she had no idea.

# CHAPTER 65

As Nadine lay in the warm bed, it belied her confused, frightened state of mind. She worried who her captors were, what they knew about her, what they wanted, and worse yet, what they would do to her or with her. After hours of tortured thinking, she reconciled herself to the fact that without her cell phone she had lost control of her life. Others now controlled her. There was nothing she could do to change that.

She tried to take solace in the fact that during the twenty-two appropriations she performed, no one was killed or suffered so much as a single scratch. She hoped that was something in her favor. Something else in her favor. She appropriated money only from the arrogant rich with sums not likely to cause economic hardship.

Over the years, she came to the realization it wasn't the money that had the arrogant rich in such an uproar. It was their precious baubles: junk they seldom if ever wore or even took out of their secret hiding places. *Not so secret,* she laughed. She had appropriated them, hadn't she? How safe was that? *Not very,* she mused to herself.

# CHAPTER 66

The deep, restorative sleep Nadine craved evaded her. She tossed and turned. Images of the hole filled her thoughts. Time stood still as she looked at the clock on the table next to the bed. Only a minute had passed since the last time she looked at it.

With no hope of sleep, she decided to focus on the high points of her life. A brief smile came to her lips as she recalled the look on her parents' faces when they saw her dressed for the prom, and then there was the incredibly handsome Tommy Ward who became speechless when he saw her: the once frizzy-haired Nadine Car.

Nadine sat straight up in bed. "That damned frizzy hair," she muttered out loud. The mind realized she had been photo ID'd: that someone, somewhere had found a picture of her with frizzy hair. The mind thought hard. It could think of just two places where such a photo might exist: her high school yearbook and the police tape of the raid at the locksmith's shop.  As the mind digested this information, it realized CC hadn't captured her but the Kansas City Police.  Then the mind had a second thought.  The Kansas City Police wouldn't spend money on a five-star hotel.  It deduced her captors were the FBI.

Nadine gained great comfort from these thoughts.  She realized she no longer had to fear being thrown in a hole that the FBI was on a fishing expedition: that they considered her nothing more than a person of interest with information that might lead to other crimes.  Yes.  It was information they wanted: nothing more.  This one thought made her feel in control.  Relief flooded her body as the fear faded.

# CHAPTER 67

Nadine lay back and snuggled under the covers secure in the knowledge she was safe. Her tranquil mind returned to events long ago. It could still see the astonished looks on her parents' and Tommy Ward's faces when they saw her dressed for the prom. Their expressions were priceless. Ones she would never forget, but as delightful as they were, she considered prom night her greatest achievement when she fooled her classmates and the pompous Levesque into believing she was a member of the French aristocracy.

The mind next turned to appropriations. It was most proud of the first two: the Pierson-Heagle appropriations where she experienced the joy and exhilaration of having control, of having manipulated, and of having inflicted serious psychological trauma upon the hypocritical rich. These appropriations confirmed the fact that hurting others gave her more sexual gratification than Tommy Ward's sweaty hands fumbling with her breasts ever had.  What she still couldn't understand was why were her associates so concerned about trinkets that had to be heavily insured?  Why didn't they collect the insurance money and be done with it?

The mind, tired of thinking about past appropriations, recalled a magnificent performance of the Berlin Symphony Orchestra that had given stirring renditions of classical favorites it could still hear so many years later.  After the concert, she had dined at an exclusive club for a late night, sumptuous supper. She tried to block out what happened afterward, but the mind wouldn't let go of the events that were soon to transpire.

# CHAPTER 68

It was a beautiful late summer evening with the smell of flowers heavy in the air. *A perfect night for a stroll in the moonlight,* so Nadine thought as she strolled through a small park on her way back to the hotel. Suddenly, two men jumped from behind bushes and threw her to the ground. Instinctively, she screamed as loud as she could. One tried to put his hand over her mouth, but she managed to bite him so hard he removed it. The other man managed to rip off her panties and was in the process of unzipping his pants when quite by accident one of her flailing stiletto heels caught him in the crotch. The frustrated, angry men kicked her head and torso. She could taste hot gushes of blood in her mouth as she gasped for air.

Through the haze, she heard a deep male voice shout, *"Halt! Halt!"* The voice frightened the attackers who fled into obscurity. A man helped her to her feet and offered to take her to a hospital.  Between gasps of bloody breaths, she had the presence of mind to say she would contact private help.  The unbelieving man remained by her side convinced she should go to a hospital for medical treatment and report the attempted rape to the police.  She activated her CC code and requested an ambulance.  The mind could still remember the surprised look on the man's face when an ambulance appeared in less than five minutes.  As the ambulance raced to a CC hospital, she lapsed into unconsciousness.  It was several days before she could leave the hospital.

Once she regained her strength, she decided to follow in Betty's footsteps.  She enrolled in martial arts classes.  Within several months her body was rock hard, and within two years of hard training, she earned her black belt.

Several years later in Rio, she demonstrated what a black belt could do when three young hooligans attacked her hoping to steal her valuables along with her virtue.  In less than a minute, all three lay unconsciousness on the sidewalk.  Unruffled by the attack, she slowly walked back to the hotel with her handbag slung over her right shoulder.

The nice warm bed finally lolled the mind into tranquility.  The body relaxed.  The mind lapsed into dreamless sleep.

# CHAPTER 69

adine jerked awake. She looked at the clock on the table: 10:41. Her first thoughts brought fear. Why hadn't there been a knock at the door for breakfast? She noticed for the first time a blue bathrobe draped over a chair. She quickly slipped it on and rushed to the door fearing it would be locked. When she opened it, she saw a man sitting in the living room hunched over his laptop.

The man looked up and in a friendly voice said, "Good morning. I've been waiting for you to wake up. Hungry?"

Nadine nodded her head *yes.*

The man picked up the house phone and ordered breakfast. When he had finished, he turned to her and said, "You're free to move about the apartment, but you can't leave it. Understood?"

Nadine nodded her head *yes.* She returned to the bedroom and waited for breakfast to arrive. A few minutes later, she was eating scrambled eggs, bacon, pancakes, buttered toast, and a pot of coffee with an array of sweeteners and containers of cream.   Although a non-meat-eater, she had learned from experience: when in captivity eat every bite of food offered. When she finished, she carried the tray to the apartment's kitchen, returned to the bedroom, closed the door, and slipped back into her warm bed she considered her private sanctuary.

# CHAPTER 70

Now that Nadine was once again safe under the covers and properly fed, the tranquil mind drifted from one scenario to another. It finally focused on a quiet vegetarian restaurant on Wiltshire Boulevard in Beverly Hills. Nadine, dining alone, had ordered a caprese salad. While she waited for it to arrive, she thumbed through a variety of pictures, emails, news headlines, and anything else she could find of interest on her cell phone.

The restaurant's door flew open. A tall, heavy-set figure wearing a huge, over-sized red hat that partially covered the face, a gaudy, tight-fitting flowered blouse that accentuated the size of the breasts, a too tight-fitting pair of designer red jeans, and red platform shoes burst forth. The figure looked around and in a loud, brash voice said, "Christ, it's like a fuckin' morgue in here. Let's liven this dump up with some knock-knock jokes. Knock-knock," the figure said in a low voice. "Who's there?" a sweet voice asked. "Ice cream," the deep voice answered. "Ice cream who?" the sweet voice asked. "Ice cream if you don't let me in." The figure roared with laughter.

"Here's another." The figure lowered its voice and whispered, "It's kinda smutty, but ya gotta admit those are the best kind. Okay. Here goes. Knock-knock. Who's there? Banana. Banana who? Banana split so ice creamed." The figure laughed another loud, hearty laugh. "Get it? Ice creamed. Okay," the figure exhaled loudly. "Enough of that shit. Any new faces here or the same ole tired bitches." The figure looked around the dimly lit restaurant. "Ah-ha, here's somebody new." The figure took off the large hat and sat down opposite Nadine.

Nadine recognized the figure in front of her. Sassy Fras was a favorite guest on talk shows, and she had made several movies: all bad. Nadine wasn't impressed Sassy deigned to dine with her. Nevertheless, she decided she had nothing to lose by being friendly. "Hello, Sassy," she said in a friendly voice.

"What kind of rabbit shit are you havin' today?" Sassy asked without missing a beat, unimpressed the woman knew her. Who didn't? She was famous. Everybody fuckin' well oughta know her, and if they didn't, they were assholes.

"A caprese salad."

"Hey, you, the one holdin' the fuckin' tray. Ya you," Sassy yelled at a young woman who stood rooted to the spot obviously star-struck by the presence of such an important celebrity as Sassy Fras. "Get your ass over here so I can give ya ma order."

The young woman hesitantly approached the table. Sassy bellowed, "I'm havin' what she's havin'. Got it?" When the girl didn't move, Sassy turned away so the girl couldn't see her face, waited a few seconds, and then whispered to Nadine, "Is she still there?" When Nadine nodded her head *yes*, Sassy turned to the waitress and in a sarcastic tone of voice said, "I hope ta hell you can remember all that between here and the kitchen." When the young woman still didn't move, Sassy bellowed, "So why are you just standin' there doin' nothin'? Get your ass in the kitchen and fix the fuckin' salad. What's so fuckin' hard about that?" She turned her attention to Nadine, rolled her eyes, and exclaimed, "It's so fuckin' hard to get good help these days."

Nadine didn't respond but sat studying the vulgar woman in front of her. She realized without money and celebrity the waitstaff would have thrown Sassy out, but because of who she was, the star-struck staff catered to the foul-mouthed woman who considered herself clever and smart.

The mind skipped the rest of the lunch except the last few bites of the caprese salad when Sassy asked, "Are you doin' anythin' tonight?  If not, I'm havin' a little get together at my place in Malibu.  A few of my closest friends will be there, so if you like Hollywood types, you'll love my party.  Starts at midnight." She lowered her voice. "The bewitching hour." And ends?" She shrugged her shoulders and laughed out loud, "God only knows when it'll end cause these folks know how to party.  Here's my card and address.  Hope to see you there?  By the way, what's your name."

"Cynthia."

"Hope to see you there, Cindy."

Sassy turned to leave when she looked back over her shoulder and asked, "What's your last name, honey?"

"Krinkel," Nadine answered.  "Cynthia Krinkel with a K."

"Christ, what kind of an asshole name is Krinkel?  I'll just call ya Cindy.  All right?"

"Okay by me," Nadine replied as she watched Sassy disappear through the opened door.

# CHAPTER 71

As Nadine drifted in and out of consciousness, the mind recalled loud music and a haze that hung over a room. A naked woman stoned out of her mind moved about the room screaming, "I don't give a fuck what y'all think. I'm gonna do it my way." It was then Nadine felt a gentle touch on her left shoulder. A tall, young man bent down and yelled in her ear, "I think we're the only sober people here."

Nadine looked into the face of Tyler Haines voted America's sexiest man for three straight years. Even with the briefest of glances, she could see he was out of his element. She smiled a beguiling smile and nodded her head *yes.*

"I came with her," he yelled. His handsome face grimaced in disgust as he pointed to a naked female form sprawled over a coffee table. He looked about the room. When his gaze focused back on Nadine, he appeared lost as if he couldn't believe what he was seeing. He leaned close to her ear and said, "I've never been to one of these parties.  It'll be the last.  How can people waste their talents and their lives like this?"

Nadine shrugged her shoulders in response.

"Did you come with anyone?"

She shook her head *no*.

"Could we get out of here? Please?" he pleaded.

Nadine smiled and nodded her head *yes*.

Once outside the drug-infused haze, Tyler walked in circles sucking in as much salty Pacific air as he could. "Whew," he wheezed. "The air in that place is toxic." He turned to Nadine and in a forceful voice said, "I don't want to go back into that den of iniquity.  Do you have a car?"

Nadine nodded her head *yes*.

"Could you rescue a dude in distress?"

Nadine laughed and motioned for him to follow.  Once the car was headed toward Los Angeles, Tyler leaned back, looked at her, and said softly, "You've just saved one man's life."

"And you saved mine," Nadine replied.  "I needed an excuse to get out of there."

Neither spoke until they were back in LA.  Tyler looked at her and asked hopefully, "Hungry?"

"Men! That's all they ever think about: their stomachs," she retorted in a mock- serious voice, "but now that you mention it, I could use a little something to eat."

It was between bites of burger and fries that Tyler confided he was tired of being sexy. "I hereby relinquish my sex-symbol crown," he laughingly told Nadine. "I like you, Cynthia, but could we just be friends?"

Nadine smiled a coquettish smile and after a sip of her vitamin water that she always drank through a straw, said in a sexy voice, "That would be nice." With this sweet thought, the mind shut down and the tranquility of sleep overtook her.

# CHAPTER 72

Nadine yawned and stretched after a good night's sleep. As she lay in bed staring at the ceiling, wonderful thoughts of Tyler Haines's innate gentleness filled the mind. Without warning, it suddenly jumped to Sassy. It rejoiced at the thought that Nadine had waited many years to appropriate Sassy's jewelry so she would never suspect Nadine of being the appropriator who had appropriated her entire bling collection along with thousands of dollars. *Serves the filthy, no talent, big mouth right,* the mind rationalized.

Tired of Sassy, the mind wanted to have a look at the outside world. Nadine walked to the window, pulled back the heavy blue drapes, and gazed upon a city caught in the grip of a snowstorm. She closed the drapes and meandered about the room examining the pictures hanging on the walls and thinking the frames more interesting than the pictures.

She turned her attention to the expensive-looking furniture that adorned the room. It was then she spied a remote on a long table beneath the wall-mounted TV. She pressed the power button. After a minute of channel surfing, she realized it was programmed only to receive movie channels. She sat down on one of the plush chairs nearest the TV to watch a movie called *Blue Hawaii* with some guy she'd never heard of called Elvis Presley. He seemed to capture the hearts of the girls in the movie, but when Nadine heard him sing one corny song after another, she turned off the TV.

She decided to return to her sanctuary, the bed, where she let the mind rove wherever it wanted. It settled on an appropriation that if it hadn't been for quick thinking could have ended in disaster. She was walking down the associate's driveway dressed in a perfectly tailored, light-gray business suit, wearing a matching gray hat with a broad brim that cast a shadow over her face, and carrying a large over-the-shoulder gray handbag she had just stuffed with a large amount of cash and numerous pieces of jewelry when a dark SUV pulled into the driveway beside her. The driver, a woman in her mid-forties, put down the window and asked, "Can I help you?"

"Yes," Nadine replied in an aristocratic British accent knowing full well no one questioned such an accent. "The cab driver seems to have deposited me at the incorrect address. I thought this was my *ahunt's* residence. She offered to drive me to the rail station, but." She stopped mid-sentence to let the idea she was stranded sink into the woman's brain. "I can assure you such a thing would never happen in London where the drivers know every street in the city. Here…" she let her voice trail off.

"Happens all the time. This is Wellston Drive. I bet you wanted North Wellston. Hop in. I'll take you to the station."

"I couldn't…"

"Yes you can. If the stupid driver dropped you off on my doorstep, the least I can do is help you out," and so Nadine quite properly entered the vehicle being certain her short skirt in no way revealed anything that was improper to reveal.

Later, in her hotel room, she smiled at the naiveté of the woman who had unwittingly been an accomplice to her own appropriation. *Never underestimate a British accent,* Nadine laughed to herself, recalling her hastily concocted story about an aunt that made no sense.

# CHAPTER 73

Lunch arrived. Nadine was pleased it included a large spinach salad with olive oil on the side and lots of fresh fruit. She hadn't enjoyed the salty breakfast bacon. It made her incredibly thirsty, forcing her to drink too much water. *Good way to put on weight,* she thought to herself.

As she munched on her lunch, the mind questioned why no one had come to interrogate it. It arrived at two possibilities: the snowstorm and her cell phone. It reasoned the interrogator wasn't in Kansas City. If he-she were, they would have wasted no time interviewing it snowstorm or no snowstorm. The mind also reasoned that FBI computer specialists were examining her cell phone at that very moment. It felt confident they wouldn't be able to break the CC code. If they did, it knew Nadine as well as CC would be in serious trouble.

This last thought upset the mind. She turned on the TV in an effort to quiet it. While one stupid movie after another filled the screen, none of them registered with the mind that relived its own reality. One of its favorite recollections was the time she wore a fat suit: a disguise she particularly liked because no one paid any attention except to give her the occasional nasty look that said, not asked, *how could you let yourself get so fat!* She had waddled into the residence of a Swiss bank president while pushing a well-used upright vacuum cleaner under the pretext she was there to clean. It didn't take long to locate the safe and appropriate thousands of euros and scads of expensive looking jewelry. As a parting gift, she left the vacuum in the bedroom closet where it couldn't be overlooked. She roared at the headlines on the Internet the next day, *Thief Makes Clean Sweep,* as the article described the robbery along with a strange clue that baffled Swiss police: an old vacuum found in the middle of a walk-in closet.

The mind next turned to romance. It tried to remember how many men had romantic intentions toward her over the years. Each man, whether young or old, had become nothing more than a blur. The mind did remember their fumbling attempts to lure her into their beds from the indirect, "I would really like to know you better", to the direct, "Would you say you were more of a top than a bottom." Some were much too direct reaching for her breasts or trying to get their hand up a tight-fitting skirt.  She didn't mind so much their wanting to do this, but by invitation only, not some spur-of-the-moment gesture she was supposed to find sexually exciting: which she didn't.

As the mind drifted over the years of sexual advances, it calculated there had to be hundreds of them: too many to remember: a thought that brought a smile to her lips.  *The ice queen melts men's hearts*, ran through the mind.

# CHAPTER 74

The fear that had consumed Nadine when she first arrived at the hotel had been replaced with relief, but as the days slowly passed, relief gave way to the mixed emotions of boredom and the deep-seated fear that one day soon she might end up in a dingy prison cell or worse yet: a hole. Not knowing her fate was worse than knowing.

One morning after breakfast, she heard a soft knock on the door, a long pause, and then the door opened just wide enough for a man to put his head through the small opening. "Please be properly dressed in one hour." He backed out of the partially opened door and closed it. *Finally,* Nadine thought to herself. *I'm going to meet my captors.*

An hour later she was ushered to the spacious dining room and seated in one of two chairs at the table. She had to wait for what seemed an interminable amount of time until she heard muffled voices coming from the hallway.

Moments later a disgustingly heavy-set man entered the dining room and sat down in the empty chair. After the man seated himself, the smell of cigar smoke permeated the air. Instinctively she wrinkled her nose in disgust.

The man looked at her and without apology said, "I'm Special FBI Agent Bud Perkins and you're Nadine Car." Nadine sat quietly with her attention focused on her lap waiting for what the unattractive man had to say. "While you've been living large in this luxurious hotel, the FBI's been hard at work. It took our IT guys a while to break your CC cell phone code, but I am pleased to report to you that truth and justice have won out. I can now inform you that you are penniless or should I say crypto-coinless." He smiled at his joke. Nadine sat staring at her lap.

"All your CC funds have been confiscated and have been used to pay for your present lodgings. I can also report to you that Crypto-Coin is officially out of business. Of course, mopping up operations will continue for years to come, but CC is gone, finished, *kaput.*" Perky put special emphasis on the t in *kaput.*

He paused, waiting for Nadine either to react to what he had just told her or perhaps make some sort of statement.

She did neither. "Just to bring you up to date what's been happening since you went away, your parents are in good health. They moved from the William Walker apartments to a nice house. They have a tabby cat named Nadine, so you've not been forgotten."

He paused again for some type of reaction from her, but none was forthcoming, so he continued. "Now to business. First, I want the key Luther Wilson gave you. Second, the bureau now has half your wealth. We want the other half. I must warn you; you must tell me the absolute truth. If I catch you in one false statement, I won't hesitate to throw you in a hole so deep you'll never see the light of day again."

Nadine's body instinctively moved ever so slightly at the mention of the word *hole*. To the untrained, the movement might have gone unnoticed, but to an expert interrogator like Perky, he instantly realized the Car woman was afraid of being thrown in a dark hole. This he could use against her whenever he needed to ensure her complete cooperation.

# CHAPTER 75

Nadine hoped the fat, cigar smelling man hadn't noticed her body move at the word *hole*, but she couldn't take the chance. She knew she had zero choices. She had to comply with whatever he demanded.

"First things first. I want the key. Where is it?"

Nadine didn't hesitate to answer. Staring straight ahead at the wall opposite her, she recited in a monotone, "Safety-deposit-box 268, The Bank of KC and M, Main Street, Kansas City.

Perky got up from the table and called the bureau's Kansas City office to secure a warrant to open the safety-deposit-box. He returned to the table. "That's all for now. I'll let you know when we have the key." He paused. "For your sake, that key better be in deposit-box 268." He stood and left the apartment. Nadine sat quietly for a few minutes lost in her own thoughts. Finally, she got up and returned to her room.

# CHAPTER 76

The next morning Nadine was taken to the dining room. Moments later the stench of stale cigar smoke filled the air as the voice of the interrogator filled her ears. "Good news, Nadine. We have the key, and a good thing too. It was this close," he held his thumb and index finger close together, "to being lost forever because you hadn't paid the rent for the deposit-box. It was way past due. The Post Office had already removed it from the box. The really good news is that it's in the FBI's Washington bureau being examined by our IT guys as we speak. Okay, Ms. Car. You've passed your first test. Now for your second test. I know you committed twenty robberies. Are there any others I don't know about?"

"When I was nineteen, I committed two appropriations: Anita Pierson: a feminist professor at Purdue, and Jeremy Heagle: the Toffee King."

"Any others?"

"No."

"What did you take from each of them?"

"Money, Heagle's Rolex, and jewelry from both."

"Did you fence any of their jewelry or jewelry you stole in the other twenty robberies?"

"No."

"Where's the jewelry now?"

"In deposit-boxes."

"Now for your third and final test." Perky shoved a yellow legal pad in front of her along with a pen. "I want you to write down each person's name you robbed. I want the names of the banks and deposit-box numbers where the jewelry is. I leave you to your homework."

In less than thirty minutes, Nadine made a list of associates, their safety-deposit-box numbers along with the names of the banks where the jewelry was stored. When Perky looked at the list written in neat cursive handwriting, he asked gruffly, "You're absolutely positive you've left no one off the list and the deposit-box numbers are correct?"

"Yes."

"One last question.  Besides this key," he held it up for Nadine to see, "did you do anything else to gain entry into the homes of the rich and famous."

"I wore disguises."

"I see.  Okay, Ms. Car, you can return to your room while we check out this information," he held up the legal pad, "to be certain the jewelry is where you say it is." Perky got up from the table and left the apartment while Nadine returned to her room.

# CHAPTER 77

By Nadine's count, she hadn't seen the cigar-smoking FBI agent for twenty-nine days. On the thirtieth day, she was taken to the dining room where the foul-smelling cigar-smoker was already seated. He began speaking once she sat down. "You passed your third test. It took a while to pry the jewelry out of the hands of the banks: especially the European and Swiss banks. All pieces have been accounted for."

He continued speaking in a non-threatening voice. "I'm going to offer you a position, Ms. Car, to work with the combined efforts of the FBI and CIA here and abroad. You'll work for these two bureaus for as long as they deem necessary. You'll be given the most dangerous jobs. If you accept the proposition, you'll be accompanied to a small apartment in Brooklyn by a female agent who will stay with you until you receive your instructions. If you decline the offer, you'll be taken to prison. Now is the moment Ms. Car: yes or no."

With the warmest of smiles, Nadine, in a soft, sexy voice, replied, "I accept your offer."

# CHAPTER 78

Perky walked into Jocko's office at CIA headquarters. Because of his outstanding college and pro football careers, he had earned the one name. No one seemed to know his real name since everybody from the CIA director to the cleaning staff called him Jocko: a name spoken with great respect. Perky and Jocko had been friends for years so when Perky walked into Jocko's office, it was old home week. After the usual greetings, Jocko asked, "So what brings you to my neck of the woods?"

"I've got a hot property. One both of us can use."

"Sounds interesting."

"It is. I've solved a case that's baffled domestic and foreign law enforcement agencies for years, and," he paused for effect, "I have the suspect in custody."

"Ya right," Jocko burst out laughing, "and I suppose you've been up to your old interrogator tricks blowin' cigar smoke in the suspects' faces and makin' 'em confess."

"Would I sit in traffic for two hours if I didn't have the goods, and for your information, I did use the ole cigar smoke routine. God, I gotta cut cigars out of my interrogations. Them segees damned near killed me." They both laughed.

"However, I added something new to my bag of tricks. I had the prosthetic department make my face, neck, and body look disgustingly fat. The suspect was so turned off by stale cigar smoke and my disgusting appearance, it would have confessed to anything just to get rid of me."

When the laughter died down, Jocko turned serious and asked, "Why haven't I heard about this most baffling case being solved and the suspect apprehended?"

Perky got up from the chair, leaned over Jocko's desk, and spoke in a whisper to ensure no one but Jocko could hear what he was about to say. "Because no one knows I've solved the EC case, and only I know the suspect's identity. It's so top-secret I'm not even gonna tell you the suspect's name: only that the suspect's a woman. I have a specific job for her: to infiltrate the Russian mafia. Here's where you come in. I want to connect the American Russian mafia to the Kremlin to find out what the hell's goin' on behind the Kremlin's stone walls, and what they're planning for us here in America. Remember the Nazis a few years back pretending to be Moslem terrorists? I wouldn't put it past the Ruskies to do something as underhanded as that. You have connections inside the Kremlin. I need you to connect the dots so we can castrate these bastards both here and there."

Perky stepped back from Jocko's desk and waited for him to say something. When he didn't, Perky continued. "The suspect speaks fluent Russian. She's currently in training with my agents learning how to become a waitress and how not to react to anything being said in Russian. If those guys find out she speaks Russian, we'll never see her again."

Perky stopped and stared at Jocko. If there was anyone he could trust, it was Jocko. Nevertheless, he felt it necessary to remind him this was a top-secret project. "Not a word to anybody," he whispered, "especially not your blabber-mouth director."

Jocko smiled at the reference to the CIA director and said quietly, "Mum's the word."

"The suspect's going to be a waitress at the Bright Spot Diner in Brooklyn where the mafia guys hang out. They feel the diner is far enough away from their home turf so they can talk freely.  At least I hope they do, and because they talk Russian, they think no one can understand them.  I'd bug the place if I could, but the owner is a small-time drug pusher who keeps close tabs on his establishment and everyone who works for him.  One thing on our side.  The diner's owner has trouble keeping waitresses because the Russian guys treat 'em so badly.  He gladly hired the woman once he saw her, or should I say saw her disguise.  Since she's a master of disguises, I've selected her code name: Chameleon."

# CHAPTER 79

Nadine arrived at the Bright Spot a few minutes before 5 a.m. Three men sat at the counter. It was obvious they had been up all night and actively engaged in some sort of physical activity due to their disheveled appearance.

As Nadine entered the kitchen, she came face-to-face with an attractive young woman who was in the process of putting on her coat. She appeared to be in her mid-twenties. "Thanks," she said in a relieved tone of voice, "for comin' in an hour early. I told Dimetri I don't mind workin' extra hours, but I refuse to wait on them three animals at the counter, and that's what they are: animals. Seven days a week they're here, always sittin' at the counter, eatin' everything but breakfast.

"A word of warnin'." She looked around to be certain no one could hear her. In a low, frightened voice said, "All three of 'em pulled me over the counter last Tuesday, throwed me on the floor, grabbed my breasts, pulled down my panties and jumped on top of me laughin' their asses off while they done it. I hope they all rot in hell. Anyways, good luck to ya, and once again, thanks for comin' in early." She turned and went out the diner's backdoor so she wouldn't have to walk past *the three animals*.

# CHAPTER 80

Nadine had selected her waitress disguise *sloppy-careful* as she called it. She dyed her straight hair jet-black using a cheap dye that left no doubt it was a dye job. To complete her disguise, she wore a too tight pink uniform that accented her assets.

She picked up a hot carafe of coffee and walked through the kitchen's swinging doors toward the three men seated at the counter. "Good morning, gentlemen" she said in a friendly manner as she grabbed three cups from behind her.

At the sight of her, the three men made crude comments in Russian about her feminine attributes. "So, what are you gentlemen havin' for breakfast this morning?" she asked as she poured coffee.

"You!" the one in the middle said leering at her breasts. From his seated position and the deference of the two seated beside him, Nadine knew he was the headman.

"You wish."

"Whatever I wish, I get."

"The only wish you're gonna get is the food you order."

"Sos where's the fuckin' menu? You think we're fuckin' mind readers here?"

"You know the menu better than I do. You been comin' here long before I was born." The men seated beside the headman laughed but quickly quieted down when they saw he wasn't amused. Food ordered and served, the men tested her repeatedly to see if she understood Russian. This continued for several weeks until they were convinced she didn't. What really convinced them was when Nadine in an angry voice said, "This is America. Talk English. When I'm servin' ya, I don't wanna hear that jibber-jabber you're talkin'." To piss her off, the three spoke Russian, speaking English only when they wanted something.

# CHAPTER 81

Nadine entered a room where two men sat at a small table. She didn't recognize either of them. Both stood smiling as she approached them. One of the men spoke in a voice that sounded familiar, yet she couldn't place it. "Allow me to introduce this gentleman to you." He motioned to the tall, well-built man standing next to him. "His name is Jocko. He represents the CIA. Perhaps you remember his illustrious football career where he set one record after another."

"I don't follow sports," she said coldly.

"You're meeting one of the greatest legends in sports history, and you have no idea who he is?"

"He's a man. That's all I can say about him."

The man shook his head in disbelief as he motioned for Nadine and Jocko to sit while he remained standing. "I won't introduce myself," he said looking at Nadine, "because you already know me."

Nadine's eyes narrowed as she tried to recall the man standing before her. The voice was familiar, yet she couldn't connect it with anyone she knew. "I'm afraid I don't recall ever having met you," she said succinctly.

"You should. We've spent some time together. I'll give you one clue. I'm the one who's gotten you into this mess."

"That man was a fat slob who reeked of cigar smoke," she responded in a disgusted tone of voice.

Both the man and Jocko erupted in laughter. "See! I told ya, Jocko. I haven't lost my touch."

"I think you've upped your game."

Nadine sat mystified as to why these two men were having such a good laugh at her expense.

"Okay, Nadine. Joke's over. I'm the fat slob, the cigar-reeking-smoker, Special FBI Agent Bud Perkins."

For a few moments, Nadine sat stunned, then she burst into laughter: the first time Perky had seen her show any emotion. It was this first meeting that formed the bond that was to serve them well in the operations to come.

# CHAPTER 82

"Hey bitch. Get your fuckin' ass over here."

"You talkin' to me?"

"Who in the hell do you think I'm talkin' to. You're the only bitch in the place, sos I must be talkin' to your ass, so get it over here."

Nadine walked slowly to where the three men were sitting.

"We got a question," the one in the middle said. "Why you workin' seven fuckin' days a week? Don't you ever take a fuckin' day off?"

"I would if yous assholes would ever give me a tip."

The men laughed. "Ain't gonna happen, bitch. Besides, we like havin' yous here with us every mornin', smilin' that sweet smiles of yours."

"Just my luck."

"If you're really lucky, I'll wrap you around my *petukh*."
All three men smirked.

"If that means what I think it means, I'd call that a misfortune sos don't get your hopes up or anything else cause it ain't never gonna happen."

"I ain't never had no complaints.  You'd enjoy it."

"Not likely."

"We're the only people here sos there's no time like now. After I've givin' you the best fuck you ever had, you can fuck my two friends here."  The other two men grinned in anticipation.

The headman leaned over the counter to grab her.  Before he knew what had happened, he was lying on the floor staring at the ceiling.  "What the fuck?" he screamed. Moments later, he struggled to his feet while the other two men stared in disbelief. Nadine didn't know if she had just compromised her mission, but one thing she did know.  None of them would try that trick again.

# CHAPTER 83

Nadine didn't know what to expect when she entered the diner a few minutes before five. She was pleased to see the three Russians seated in their usual places. As she went about her work, she detected a change in their attitude. They hadn't greeted her with the usual sexual innuendos and filthy language in Russian and English.

The headman, before he ordered his food, looked into Nadine's eyes, and said, "I..." The words were hard to say, but for reasons of his own, he felt he had to say them even though he ran the risk of losing his comrades' respect. "I apologize for what happened yesterday. I was out of line: way out of line. It was just my way of saying I like you: a lot: which I do. It won't happen again. I promise. I want you to know the offer is always open," he said hopefully.

"Don't hold your breath," Nadine said firmly.

"And I promise to treat you like a lady."

"Yeah, right," Nadine sneered.

When the men finished eating, each left a five-dollar tip: a daily practice that continued in the weeks and months that followed.  One even bigger change occurred.  They no longer talked Russian in lowered voices: a sign she had won not just their respect but their trust.  *Men,* Nadine thought to herself.  *Russian, French, American.  Who can figure them out?*

# CHAPTER 84

The Bright Spot Diner was anything but. Not only was it a greasy, dingy dive, but the hours were long, especially for Nadine who worked a nine-hour shift and sometimes more when Evelyn arrived an hour or more late sweaty and disheveled. Nadine knew what she'd been up to: bangin' Dimetri in the storeroom.

Long hours weren't the only problem. Difficult customers, hot, heavy plates with bad pay added to the list of workplace complaints, but Nadine was in no position to complain. She had to fulfill her obligation to the two bureaus or suffer the consequences. The one bright spot was Perky allowed her to keep her wages and tips until he discovered she invested them in a Japanese virtual currency. He confiscated her pay and tips, shut down her account, and warned her if she ever tried that stunt again, she would be severely punished. Nadine knew she had no choice but to follow Perky's orders.

As for the three Russians at the counter, they spent their time bragging to each other about the underage girls they raped before coming to the diner. "Breakin' 'em in right," they gloated in Russian proud of their sexual accomplishments. They brazenly discussed the anatomies of the young girls they had raped in the crudest language possible and what would happen to them. The prettiest ones were sent to up-scale houses in Manhattan where they serviced the most influential men in New York City: Wall Street hot shots, politicians, lawyers, judges, union bosses, show business personalities, sports figures, and Fortune 500 CEOs where they earned for the syndicate anywhere from $1500 to $2,000 an hour. The least desirable girls were shipped to Jersey to work in low-class houses for a hundred a night. In time, all the girls, whether pretty or plain, suffered the same fate: an opioid overdose, death, ground up, mixed with garbage, and dumped in some municipal dump. The girls had zero chance of escaping this grisly fate.

Nadine was surprised to learn she had a social conscience. She felt no pity for her associates when she appropriated their valuables or the men whose hearts she broke, but her attitude changed as she listened to the cold, calculating comments of the three men at the counter who considered the underage girls nothing more than sex objects to be used and abused as they saw fit.  She informed Perky and Jocko of the international underage prostitution ring as well as the drug smuggling operations.  Tired of working nine plus hours a day, seven days a week, she hoped she could bring this assignment to a close so she could get out of the waitressing business.

# CHAPTER 85

To Nadine, the days at the Bright Spot seemed as if they'd never end. Another year passed and *the gang of three* as she came to call them bragged daily about their sexual escapades with underage girls, the international drug pipelines they had set up, and the extreme amounts of money their businesses made. They congratulated themselves for being such smart operatives since none of their sex or drug operations had been uncovered by *the stupid Americans* as the gang of three referred to them.

At one of their meetings, Perky assured Nadine and Jocko he had more than enough evidence to indict the Russian mafia and destroy their sex and drug trade operations. "It's time to pull the plug," he informed them, but Jocko disagreed. "I've gotten wind something big is in the offing. No idea what it is: yet." He looked at Nadine and said, "This is just my personal speculation, Nadine, but I think you could be the lynchpin in exposing more than just Russian drug and sex operations."

Both men fell silent waiting for Nadine to voice her opinion. She was slow to respond and when she did, she spoke in an emotional tone of voice. "The underage sex and drug deaths horrify me. I would like to close this case ASAP, but if Jocko thinks it's worth keeping open, I'm willing to give it the necessary time." Then in a strong voice quipped, "As long as my legs hold out."

# CHAPTER 86

A small break in the case occurred while the gang of three were slopping down their food one particularly fine morning. The man to the left of the headman said in loud voice, "Is it true it's a go in London?" The headman gave him a dirty look. Nadine passed these few words on to Perky hoping they meant something important.

Many weeks later, on a cold, rainy morning, the gang of three entered the deserted diner. They paid no attention to Nadine as they took their places at the counter. They appeared more disheveled than usual and talked in angry voices, loud enough so Nadine could plainly hear every word they said.

After considerable grousing about unnamed sources trying to steal their money, the man on the right blurted, "Those fucking bastards in the Kremlin are always sticking their fucking noses where they don't belong."

The headman groused, "We take all the risks.  They steal our money.  For what?  Sos some asshole.  In some office."  With each new thought, the angrier he became.  "Watching cars go round and round Piccadilly Circus."  He made circular motions with his hands.  "Plotting to crash the British and American economies, just so Vetrov can get rich at our expense.  It's a shit idea that'll never work, and if it did, it'd ruin our businesses.  Fuck the Kremlin.  Fuck Vetrov.  This is America."

"Yeah," the other two men shouted in agreement.

# CHAPTER 87

"Jocko, rather good of you to call old man. It's nearly teatime, so I can only spare a moment."

"You can drop the jolly ole English lingo, Sir Roger."

"I rather thought you Americans enjoyed hearing English spoken properly. It's you Americans who have managed to misappropriate the English language as given to us by Chaucer and Shakespeare."

"Never heard of 'em."

"Not surprising. You've never had a proper English education, but no time to educate you now. The kettle's at boil. To what do I owe the call?"

"Information."

Jocko and Sir Roger Fitz-Alan, General-Director of MI6, the UK's foreign counter-intelligence service, had worked together on previous cases so they knew each other well.

Both enjoyed the occasional jab at the idiosyncrasies of their counterpart's culture and language.

"Time you colonists pulled your weight."

"As per usual and then some, but thanks to you, we've kept our investigation open."

"Quite so.  Now permit me to catch you up on the latest developments.  It's a matter of considerable delicacy because it implicates Vetrov with a most nefarious scheme. He's trying to resurrect the old Crypto-Coin network.  Nasty bit of business this."

"So that's what the bastard is up to.  No wonder he's squeezing his overseas sex and drug operations.  My informant tells me there's a Russian operation underway somewhere on or near Piccadilly Circus bent on collapsing both the British and American economies.  It's a colossal money grab, and if Vetro can pull it off, he could make Crypto-Coin the world's reserve currency with him, not just the president of Russia but the financial czar of the world.  Look into it at your end but don't do anything until I've removed my informant."

"Righto, ole boy.  We'll begin our investigation straightaway.  Keep me informed as to when I can move on the information."

"Will do, Sir Roger," Jocko uttered with the utmost respect.

"Thank you, Jocko," Sir Roger replied with the same respect. "If you're able, please convey the gratitude of the British people to your informant for this most valuable piece of information."

The conversation concluded, the two men ended the call lost in thought with the knowledge gained from the shared information.

# CHAPTER 88

Two days after the conversation between Jocko and Sir Roger, a battered Salvation Army van pulled into the Bright Spot parking lot at 4:30 a.m. Six tired men stumbled into the diner and quietly ordered breakfast. A few minutes before five, the gang of three took their usual places at the counter. Nadine took their order and waited until they finished eating. As she handed them their check, she said casually, "I won't have to listen to your jibber-jabber no more. This is my last day."

Seeing six men wearing Salvation Army uniforms seated nearby, the gang of three restrained themselves. The headman asked, "Where ya goin'?" Then it dawned on him. "Hey! We don't know your name. So what is it?"

"As if I'd tell you. Alls I can say is, we'll never meet again, and even that'll be too soon."

Dejected at the news, the gang of three quietly left the diner but not after leaving unusually large tips their way of saying they would miss her.

As the day wore on, Nadine noticed the diner was busier than normal mostly with men and women wearing Salvation Army uniforms. "So why all yous Army people here?" Nadine asked one of the women.

"Haven't you heard?  Big prayer meetin' at the armory. God's army's gotta eat too, ya know."

Nadine shrugged her shoulders at the news and wondered why she hadn't heard about such a large prayer meeting.

# CHAPTER 89

Nadine left the diner after her usual nine-hour shift and returned to her low-rent apartment to find a female agent waiting for her. "Welcome home," she said kindly. Nadine noticed suitcases by the door. The agent responded with, "Yes, those are yours. Agent Perkins is waiting for you downtown."

Nadine found Perky in his cramped office. He offered her the only chair located behind a cluttered desk while he stood. "I understand you had a busy day hustlin' grub for all those Salvation Army folks. I hope they tipped you well, but they really shouldn't have since they're on the government payroll: FBI agents all. I couldn't take the risk the Russians might get rough so I made sure they couldn't. Hope you don't mind. Oh, by the way, before I forget, the bureau thanks you for these." He reached into his coat pocket and pulled out three one-hundred dollar bills. "Compliments of the Russians. One of the Salvation Army gentlemen seated near the Ruskies liberated the bills before you could."

Nadine smiled and, in a voice, filled with quiet respect said, "Thank you."

"My...oh...my!" Perky drew out each word slowly. "Gratitude from Agent Car herself. I wasn't expecting that. Give me a moment to digest this glorious moment." He beamed from ear-to-ear, but when he looked into Nadine's eyes, he saw she wasn't amused. "Okay. Okay. Have it your way. No humor: just business. Incidentally, before I forget," he said unable to keep excitement out of his voice, "the information you gleaned from the Russians has been invaluable. The British government and its people thank you for the service you've rendered them. So," he said with great enthusiasm, "you deserve a vacay, and a vacay you shall have. An all-expense-paid trip to the South of Spain to bask in the sunshine for the next three months. After that, I can't promise you anything except one thing. Keep your ears to the news. All hell is about to break loose, and I wouldn't want you to miss a minute of it because you're the one who's caused it. *Bon voyage.*

# CHAPTER 90

Nadine did as Perky directed her. She basked in the sun. *I wasn't cut-out to be a waitress,* ran through the mind as she lay on the crowded beach.

As the end of her three-month vacation approached, Nadine had one big disappointment. She followed Perky's advice and listened eagerly for news related to her activities with the Russians, but none was forthcoming.

The afternoon before she was to leave Spain, a man in muddy work-clothes appeared at the door. He instructed her to be ready the next morning at 6 a.m. Having delivered his message, he returned to his battered truck and drove away. The anonymous man and his message struck fear in Nadine's heart, but she had no choice. She had to follow orders.

Promptly at 6 a.m., a car appeared. She was taken to a deserted airfield a few miles from where she was staying. A Lear jet awaited her arrival. As soon as the plane's door closed, a young man wearing an expensive business suit ushered her to a luxurious, leather armchair and strapped her in. Once secured, the plane raced down the runway to takeoff.

An hour later, the plane landed in Madrid where she boarded a 747. Nine hours later the 747 landed in New York where Perky met her. "Sorry about the secrecy," were his first words.

"You scared the living delights out of me," Nadine replied in an angry voice as they climbed into the waiting Suburban.

"I apologize for the cloak-and-dagger approach, but it can't be helped. The less you know about operations the safer you are. Enough said about that. I've got another job for you just as big as the Bright Spot gig."

As the car wended its way through the heavy New York traffic, Nadine turned to Perky. "One question. I waited all summer *for all hell to break loose*. Those were your exact words, but not a word: nothing."

Perky laughed. "Be patient, my dear Nadine. It's in the works. You of all people should know these things take lots of time until every i is dotted and every t crossed."

# CHAPTER 91

**P**erky had his own set of problems ever since Uhler became FBI Director. The scuttlebutt around the bureau was the president appointed him director of the FBI solely to further the aims of corrupt domestic and international politicians as well as business interests. Scuttlebutt soon became fact as Uhler refused to investigate let alone indict those guilty of high crimes and misdemeanors. Although he earned some respect from Perky with regard to the Luther Wilson Case, he still remained a person who couldn't be trusted with sensitive information. His replacement, Director Krull, was quickly replaced for doing her job: ridding the bureau of incompetents, political informants, and bringing to justice those individuals guilty of criminal behavior.

Krull's replacement, Maurice Pangle, was selected by the president on behalf of international crime syndicates to continue the work begun by Uhler: the corruption and ultimate destruction of the FBI as an independent investigatory branch of the federal government. No one inside the bureau could trust Pangle with the exception of his dog and a few fleas. Uhler and Pangle placed Perky in an untenable position: either accept corrupt policies or go rogue and work outside the bureau's purview whenever possible.

Nadine was Perky's secret rogue project. He not only had to protect her from external threats, he also had to hide her from the bureau's internal affairs department. She was too valuable an asset to lose.

Jocko at CIA and Sir Roger at MI6 faced similar problems: the corruption of their departments. Like Perky, over the years they established an underground network of individuals inside and outside their departments whom they could trust that permitted them to embark on covert activities without the knowledge of their subordinates or superiors. All three knew if their illegal activities were ever exposed, they would not only lose their jobs, their pensions, their freedom, but perhaps their lives and be branded forever as traitors. These were dangerous times Sir Roger likened to the 1789 French Revolution when fear replaced reason.

# CHAPTER 92

Nadine's plane landed in New York on a Friday. Perky gave her the weekend to rest in a fashionable midtown hotel. At 10:00 Monday morning, she entered the private office of Luis Sanchez. Perky had contracted Sanchez to instruct her in the trading of commodities and currencies. Sanchez warned Perky that it would take months to train her properly and at considerable cost because of the complexities of making trades in domestic and international markets. Perky considered the cost acceptable if he could financially cripple radical terrorist operations.

"Good morning, Ms. Johnson," Luis said in a condescending voice as Nadine entered his office. "May I call you Sharon?" He tried to sound friendly, but the woman standing in front of him was what he considered *a complete and total disaster* wearing clothes more appropriate for a much younger woman than an older woman in her late forties or early fifties.  Nadine adopted the disguise so Sanchez would focus on two subjects: commodities and currencies and to further put him off answered in a shrill, annoying voice.  "Of course," she replied flippantly.  "Can I call you Luis?"

"Yes," he replied unenthusiastically.  *This broad has no chance,* raced through his brain.  He decided to stick to commodities and currencies so he could get rid of her sorry ass as soon as possible.

# CHAPTER 93

Two days into the training session, Luis realized that Sharon wasn't as stupid as she looked and sounded. As for Sharon's part, she said as little as possible so as not to interrupt Luis's or her concentration. In less than a month, she completed the training and was ready for service. Luis was surprised at his own emotions. Instead of being glad he no longer had to work with this *impossible* woman, he realized how much he enjoyed teaching her, how much he admired her receptivity to new ideas, and how much he respected her quickness in grasping and executing complex mathematical calculations with regard to trading.

There was something else disconcerting about this Johnson woman. Not only was she smart, but she had sex appeal. Luis prided himself on having sex only with attractive women, and yet he had sexual feelings toward an unattractive woman who on the street or in a club he wouldn't have given a second glance let alone a first.

This shook his value system. Maybe he was looking in all the wrong places for lasting love. Maybe beauty *was* only skin deep. Maybe he should be looking at women differently, not as sex objects but as intelligent human beings: a lesson he never learned. Luis wasted his life chasing beauty mistaking lust for love. As the years passed, he had sex with many beautiful women. Only the most recent ones he remembered, but Sharon Johnson remained the most remarkable woman he ever met: never forgotten.

# CHAPTER 94

Perky and Jocko met with Nadine to inform her of the newest operation: a currency scam. After a few moments of pleasantries, Perky said, "I want to thank you for saving the bureau *beaucoup* dollars by completing your training in record time. I'm afraid you upset Mr. Sanchez. He planned to get rich at our expense. Anyhow, this next operation should be easy for you. You're to be an aloof bitch."

"Of course."

"Nadine, I was kidding."

"I wasn't."

Once Perky and Jocko stopped laughing, Jocko became serious as he outlined the scam. "You'll be based in Paris. Agents will arrange a meeting between you and leaders of the Caliphate." The look on Jocko's face revealed his innermost concerns. "I won't sugar-coat the operation, Nadine. It's dangerous. You'll be dealing with highly volatile individuals ready to kill at a moment's notice if they suspect anything wrong. That's why you have one hour to complete the mission. If it's not completed by then, you're to abort: not one, single minute more."

"How soon do you want to start?"

Jocko looked at Perky. Both shrugged their shoulders. Jocko spoke. "We thought we'd leave that up to you."

"I'll need tutors for Arabic dialects along with a refresher course in Middle Eastern customs and social mores. Give me a month. I'll be ready by then."

# CHAPTER 95

Nadine, dressed in a perfectly-tailored, blue, pin-striped business suit that said *look and admire, but don't touch*, welcomed four Middle Eastern gentlemen into the suite of the five-star hotel in Paris. She greeted them in Arabic and motioned for them to seat themselves either on a small couch or straight-chairs assembled around a glass table upon which an elegant display of beautifully hand-crafted cups and saucers with matching carafes for coffee and tea along with the condiments for each had been placed.

She asked each gentleman which refreshment he preferred. She poured each one with a steady hand. She knew the gentlemen would be watching her every move to see if her hand shook in the slightest. If it did, her life would not just be in danger but perhaps ended. She spoke as she poured the coffees and teas changing topics only to ask if the individual took his coffee or tea with or without cream, sugar, or lemon.

"Gentlemen, my associates have contacted you because you are in great need of our assistance. Our time together is limited so you must either accept or decline their offer within the hour." Nadine continued speaking as she poured herself a cup of tea and sat in one of the straight chairs. "Of course, you gentlemen realize your dream of a Caliphate is at present and into the foreseeable future an unrealizable dream. It's no secret you've lost bases of operation in Afghanistan, Iraq, Syria, Libya, and Somalia: losses that have put you in a most desperate situation. For this reason, you have been forced to resort to unreliable individuals who are unable to deliver the disruptions to various governments that would destroy their ability to function." She stopped to ask each gentleman if his coffee or tea was to his taste. They nodded their approval.

"Several months ago," she continued, "your organization received two-hundred million in American dollars." She pressed a button and the wall mounted television switched on. "The names you see are the contributors to your organization, their countries of origin, and how much each has contributed." She could see shock and disbelief on the gentlemen's faces that she possessed such sensitive information. "I realize this information is extremely sensitive. No one outside of this room will ever see it. Once you received the funds," she continued, "the world's banking and financial institutions froze your accounts making it impossible for you to liquidate your assets to complete planned projects. At this moment, you have two-hundred millions and nowhere to spend them."

"How do you know so much about our transactions?"

"Information is my business."

"How can we trust you?"

"You can't: just as I can't trust you. Both parties are untrustworthy, but that's the nature of our business. I'm certain you gentlemen are in agreement." She paused as she refilled the men's empty cups with the proper refreshment and condiment. "However," she said as she delicately placed a lump of sugar in one of the teacups, "I must stress the fact that my associates contacted you gentlemen. As I said before, they are in a position to help you by becoming an intermediary that can unlock your funds for immediate use."

She poured herself another cup of tea and studied the gentlemen's expressions. She could see they were distrustful, but interested. "My associates," she continued, "offer a virtual currency that will allow you to apply your funds toward the projects you envision. Our currency operates on a private network, which is why we contacted you and why it is impossible for you to contact us. This ensures no third party can intervene in a transaction and no government can trace or tax it. Once you have invested in our virtual currency…"

"What is the name of this currency?" one of the gentlemen interrupted.

"It's virtual: henceforth nameless: just as you gentlemen are nameless to me and I to you. Please. No more interruptions. Time is scarce." She glared a steely stare that said, *interrupt me again and the deal is off.*

"Here's what our currency can do for you gentlemen," she continued in a soft tone of voice meant to assuage the gentlemen's concerns. "Our return on monies invested has ranged as low as several percent during severe market downturns and as high as many thousands of percent when markets rebounded. Our investments, incidentally, are the first to return to financial health once a financial crisis has passed. It is true you can get higher returns on your investment if you invest in other virtual currencies." She pressed a button and a line chart appeared on the television that showed the fluctuations of various currencies over a twenty-five-year period.

"As you can see, our currency, represented in blue on the chart, is far more stable than the others.  In the short-term, the other currencies outperform our currency, but in the long-term, a stable currency not only provides a steady income in good as well as bad economic times but provides a greater return for every dollar or Euro invested.  Now to the added benefits of our currency no other currency can offer.

"Unlike other currencies, you will be able to use your investment dollars to purchase directly from my associates the supplies necessary to carry out planned projects.  Guns, ammunition, gases, all types of explosives properly assembled are ready upon demand. I'm certain you've become increasingly annoyed with amateur bomb-makers who blow themselves up in some dingy apartment or mal-functioning bombs that explode without killing anyone but the freedom-fighter.  It's not only a waste of valuable resources, but it gives your organization a bad name.  Our professional bomb makers can eliminate amateur bomb makers with professional grade explosives that detonate when they're supposed to with maximum effect.

"In addition to these benefits, our currency offers one more benefit that no other currency can duplicate." She paused to take a sip of tea.  "Information," she said matter-of-factly replacing the cup in the saucer. "Our experts will provide step-by-step plans for the destruction of targets with a one to ten rating system. Eight to ten are the riskiest of all the projects because they include private residences of world leaders, key government offices, dams, electrical systems, nuclear reactors, etc. Four to seven are medium risk targets such as communication and travel centers serving as the primary targets. One to three are low risk targets with minimum value such as using trucks or exploding pressure cookers to inflict damage on anyone or anything within their immediate proximity. These methods of operation result in low mortality rates and are, therefore, hardly worth the effort. As you know all too well, the public has gotten used to these types of incidents and have learned to live with them. Of course, you want the most bang for your buck as they say in English, so my associates recommend the eight to ten category.

"If you gentlemen invest your funds with my associates, you can withdraw your money within a specified time range. Your cell phone will receive a ping and light up every fifteen minutes which will give you a fifteen second window to either invest more funds or withdraw funds. After fifteen seconds, the connection will be severed, and the password changed. Once again, this opportunity will occur every fifteen minutes twenty-four hours a day. If you don't want your cell phone pinging every fifteen minutes, you can silence the pings and use just the light.

"Now follow me gentlemen." She took them to what had once been the bedroom but in its current state was filled with weapons and drug samples. "These are the weapons at your disposal. I must warn you. Our prices are higher than the usual arms seller because our weapons are top grade with immediate delivery to your desired destination."

She pointed to small bags and vials on a table next to the grenade launchers. "Our drugs are of the highest quality. What you do with them after you have received them is at your discretion. You may spend the next thirty minutes examining and sampling the products. Once you have finished, I will need either a confirmation or a rejection of your intentions before you leave this room. If you decide to invest with us, I will give each of you a card with a one-time password so your cell phones can be activated with a ping and a light every fifteen minutes. All two-hundred millions must be deposited no later than three hours from the moment you gentlemen leave this room. If we do not receive your funds in that timeframe, the offer is cancelled and will never be offered again."

The gentlemen carefully examined the weapons and sampled the drugs. Each felt the effects from the small quality of drugs they consumed when they heard, "Time is up gentlemen. Do I have a confirmation or a rejection of the terms?"

The gentlemen nodded in agreement. "We confirm the transaction."

"Thank you, gentlemen." She handed each a card with the password. "Now I must bid you *adieu* as the French say." Quietly the gentlemen filed out of the suite.

Nadine was pleased at how well the transaction had gone. Her hours spent breaking into the radical groups backers and finances had paid off handsomely. Her only disappointment was the time wasted with Sanchez learning about trading commodities and currencies little of which she used. Still, she rationalized: all learning is worthwhile.

# CHAPTER 96

Minutes after the four Middle Eastern gentlemen left the suite, Nadine removed the red-haired wig, the blue, six-inch high-heels and stuffed them in a duffel bag along with the blue pinned-stripped business suit. She removed all cosmetics from her face along with the false eyelashes. She reached into her purse and pulled out the brown contacts her parents had bought her so many years ago. As she placed them in her eyes, they didn't seem real. They belonged to a life long ago: if that life ever existed. *No time for sentimentality,* she told herself. She messed her brackish-colored hair to look as if she had just gotten out of bed and slipped into a wrinkled, oversized purple dress and a pair of worn, brown flats.

Her cell phone sounded. That was the signal to open the door so the weapons and drugs along with the duffel bag could be removed from the suite. When the men entered, she was surprised how scruffy they looked: more like street ruffians than

CIA agents.  One of the men asked, "You all right, Chameleon?" She nodded in the affirmative.

She rode the elevator to the hotel's main lobby, exited through the revolving door, and caught a taxi that took her to the Charles de Gaulle Airport where she boarded a flight to New York.  She was greatly relieved the four Middle Eastern gentlemen were nowhere in sight.

# CHAPTER 97

Jocko sat in a room on the outskirts of Paris along with an IT specialist waiting for the Middle Eastern gentlemen to invest their money in his non-existent virtual currency. The specialist sent pings every fifteen minutes with no response. He and Jocko crossed their fingers as the last ping at the three-hour deadline was sent. Seconds later two-hundred-million-dollars flowed into their non-existent virtual currency.

Jocko knew the Middle Eastern gentlemen would test the system. Fifteen minutes later the specialist sent a ping. There was no response. Another fifteen minutes passed and another ping. Moments later a request came for a one-hundred-thousand-dollar withdrawal. The specialist looked at Jocko who without hesitation said, "I'm feeling generous today. We have two-hundred-millions of their dollars so let's send them a bonus of twenty-thousand to show our interest rates can compete with the other crypto currencies."

The specialist laughed as he sent the one-hundred-twenty-thousand dollars. At the next fifteen-minute-interval, the one-hundred-twenty-thousand dollars was reinvested in Jocko's virtual non-existent virtual currency. Unfortunately for the Middle Eastern gentlemen, they never received another ping.

# CHAPTER 98

Perky and Jocko faced a serious financial problem: what to do with two-hundred million-dollars. They realized they were obligated to turn the money over to their respective departments. They also realized if they did this, they would have to explain where the money came from, how the money had been confiscated, and why their superiors hadn't been notified of the operation. If they complied with these requests, not only would they jeopardize their own careers but Nadine's as well.

Like any criminal enterprise, Jocko wired money to bank havens throughout the world in hopes of hiding its existence, yet he knew agents sooner or later would be able to trace the money to its owners and arrest him along with Perky and possibly Nadine. How long that would take was anyone's guess. The three of them were now criminals: enemies of the state.

# CHAPTER 99

Nadine awaited her next assignment in a five-star hotel in Midtown Manhattan along with a female FBI agent. Nadine assumed the one-hour Middle Eastern operation wasn't going to earn her an all-expense paid vacay to some place warm and extravagant. All she could do was kick back and enjoy the good life as long as it lasted.

The good life came to an end when Perky and Jocko arrived nine days later. She noticed a distinct change in both of them. They didn't seem as sure of themselves as they had been just before the Middle Eastern operation, nor did they joke around as they had previously. Something had changed them. They should have been pleased the operation had gone smoothly and so much money confiscated.

It was this last thought that revealed a possible answer to their changed behavior. *What have they done with the money?* the mind wondered. Then it realized: *they've stolen it.* These thoughts greatly worried Nadine because if Perky and Jocko were in trouble, she could be too. Nevertheless, she had to do whatever they ordered her to do.

Upon seeing Nadine, Perky and Jocko neither hugged nor shook her hand because they knew she didn't like displays of emotion or physical contact so they gave her muted verbal praise. "Jocko and I congratulate you on a job well-done," Perky said quietly,

"*Merci*," she replied unemotionally, motioning for them to be seated.

"How's your Chinese?" Perky asked, taking a seat on the sofa.

"A little rusty," she admitted.

"Your next assignment will require a working knowledge of the language."

"I see. Give me the usual month refresher courses. That'll give you enough time to create my backstory. We both should be ready by then."

"True enough," Perky replied. "Now to the question of the day. How are you with children?"

"Don't know. Never had any."

Perky smiled at the factual answer. "How would you like to be nanny to the Chinese ambassador's children? A ten-year-old boy and a seven-year-old girl." He waited for some response from Nadine. When she said nothing, he added, "They're spoiled rotten and have earned the reputation of being little terrors."

"When do I start?"

"Whenever you feel you're ready, let me know, and I'll make the appointment so you can apply for the position." He looked at Jocko and said, "Fill her in on the details."

Jocko explained the information he needed and warned her to be extremely cautious. "Ambassador Chen is a dangerous man. He may appear charming, but if he has even an inkling you have knowledge of high-level plans, he won't hesitate to send you to China from whence you'll never return."

"I see it's business as usual," Nadine said coldly.

# CHAPTER 100

Nadine arrived at the Chinese embassy in upper Manhattan for her afternoon appointment looking frumpy in a shapeless purple dress, scuffed brown flats, black-framed glasses, brown contacts, and straight hair that hung lifelessly about her face. A male attaché answered the door. When she introduced herself, he bowed and said, "The ambassador is expecting you." He ushered her to the study where the ambassador awaited her arrival. "Miss Dalton, Sir," the attaché said in a quiet voice, bowed, backed slowly out of the room, and closed the door.

"Sit down, sit down, Miss Dalton," the ambassador said in a friendly tone of voice. "I understand you wish to become nanny to my two charming children. Before I can admit you into my household, I must ask you some questions."

"Of course," Nadine replied coldly.

"What is your complete name?"

"Mildred Claire Dalton. I'm forty-four years of age: never convicted of a crime."

"Yes, I see," the ambassador said as he scrolled through her information. "Wonderful invention this cell phone. It used to take days if not weeks to find information that's now available in seconds."

"I'm pleased you've discovered it," Nadine replied drily. She could see by the sudden change of expression on the ambassador's face he didn't appreciate her sarcasm.

He stared at her intently to make it clear he was her superior and that she must be subservient to his will. "Do you have any references?" he asked in a superior tone of voice.

"None," Nadine answered without hesitation.

"None?" the ambassador's voice rose in disbelief. "Have you any experience with children?"

"None."

"None? Do you like children?"

Nadine learned forward in her chair so as to be more confrontational with the ambassador. "I do not."

Her honesty took him by surprise. He sat stunned for a few moments before he asked in a gruff voice, "Why do you want this job?"

"Because I need the money.  Why else would I be here?"

"Can you at least speak Chinese?"

"No."

"I can hardly see how I can entrust my children to someone with no experience, who doesn't like children, and who can in no way enrich their lives by speaking to them in Chinese." He rose from the chair signaling the interview was over.

Nadine leaned back in the chair.  "Now let me ask you some questions before I consider this thankless job."

The ambassador glared at her.

"Do your children treat you and your wife with respect?  Do they show any respect for your position as Chinese Ambassador to the United States?  Do they show any affection toward you or your wife?  Are they respectful to those who enter your home whether they be diplomatic representatives or tradespeople?  I too have a cell phone."  She reached into her pocket and produced it.  "I too do research, and I know for a fact you've had nine different nannies since you arrived in the United States two years ago.  You've got serious child problems, and you have no solutions."

The ambassador sank slowly back into the chair.

She scrolled her cell phone until she found what she was looking for. "These are anonymous statements about the behavior of your children from various individuals who have entered your home. 'The Chen children are arrogant, snotty little brats.' Here's another. 'The Chen children are an embarrassment to the Chinese Ambassador to the US.' And another. 'The Chen children are little stinkers who need a good spanking.' And one final one. 'I dread going to the Chen house where I am disrespected by the Chen children whom I consider little terrorists.'"

"If you're looking for a sweet-sugary type, don't employ me. Your children do not need her. They need a bitch like me." She saw the ambassador recoil in his chair shocked at the word *bitch*. "Plain language is needed so you and I understand each other perfectly. No holds barred. You do your job, and I'll do mine without any interference from you, your wife, or any member of your staff. I'll accept this position only under those conditions. Do you understand my conditions?"

"Yes, but I..."

"No buts.

Nadine stood, assuming the position of power. "Give me one week. If your children do not show marked improvement by that time, I will resign my position with forfeiture of any monies owed me. Am I to have this position or not?"

"I...I don't know. I'll have to talk it over with my wife."

"Nonsense. As ambassador, you're supposed to make difficult decisions quickly. This is one of those decisions. If the answer is yes, you will show me to my room. If the answer is no, I will leave your home immediately never to return. Yes or no, Mr. Ambassador?"

The ambassador rose from the chair. "I'll have my attaché collect your belongings if you'll be so kind as to give me the address."

"Before I do that, it must be agreed upon that I will have Thursdays and Sundays off midnight to midnight. Do you agree?"

"I do, if you agree to surrender your cell phone."

"Agreed." Nadine handed him a disposable cell phone she had purchased the day before along with a neatly folded piece of paper with the address written in script and handed it to the ambassador.

The ambassador impressed by the handwriting said softly, "Permit me to escort you to your room."

# CHAPTER 101

Nadine had been in her room for just a few minutes when the door burst open and two children came bounding through it. The boy screamed, "I know your name. And you don't know mine."

"And you don't know mine," the girl said in an uncertain voice.

Nadine walked toward them and in a threatening voice said, "You may know my name, but you will never say it."

"Wanna bet? I'll say what I want, and there's nothing you can do about it. Mildred, Mildred," he shouted.

Nadine stood in front of him and began pushing him toward the open door with the pressure of her body against his. His sister watched in fascination her eyes growing wider as the spectacle before her unfolded.

"You can't touch me. I'll tell my father you're a child abuser."

Nadine pushed the boy out of the room and into the hallway. Fearing a loss of power in front of his sister, the boy took several steps back and rushed toward her with his head down. It was a simple task for Nadine to take his arm and flip him over on his back.

His sister gasped as she gazed at her brother flat on his back in the hallway. Stunned, it took the boy several moments to recover his senses. When he did, he got up and ran down the stairway shouting "Child abuser, child abuser," just as a Chinese official entered the main downstairs hallway.

The ambassador rushed from his study at the cries of his son. The boy ran to his father and explained in Chinese what the new nanny had just done to him. The ambassador said harshly in English, "Do as you are told!"

Ambassador Chen turned to the official and explained in Chinese, "New nanny," whereupon the official replied, "Child not accustomed to firm hand." Both men bowed to each other and adjourned to the study for further conversation.

# CHAPTER 102

adine closed the door to her room and began to unpack her suitcases when the door burst open. The boy entered the room while the little girl waited in the hallway peeking through the opened door not certain what to expect. "Bet you don't know my name," the boy taunted Nadine.

"I don't, and I don't want to know. You are a nasty little boy. You do not deserve to have a name. I will call you boy." She looked into the hallway at the little girl and said, "And I will call you girl. You will call me ma'am. Do you understand?"

"I'll call you any name I want," the boy replied defiantly.

Nadine pressed her body against his and pushed him into the hallway whereupon she flipped him onto his back. When he had sufficiently regained his senses, she looked down at him and in a harsh tone of voice said, "How unfortunate you're a such dull child," a refrain she was to repeat numerous times daily.

# CHAPTER 103

Before Nadine lay down for a nap prior to dinner that was served at nine o'clock due to the ambassador's busy schedule, she inquired about the children's bedtime. An attaché informed her bedtime was decided by the children which, he explained, was customary in aristocratic Chinese homes.

Nadine had just awakened from a short nap a few minutes past eight when the boy crashed through the door screaming "I hate you" along with "I'm going to kill you." He made a scary face and waved his hands clutched like claws close to her face. "Tonight!"

Nadine rose from the bed and stared a malevolent stare. The boy backed away and screamed, "I hate you" followed by "I'm going to kill you. Tonight!"

"You'll do no such thing. Stop talking nonsense."

"It's not nonsense. I'm going to kill you. Tonight."

Nadine moved toward him as he slowly backed toward the open door. "Not if I kill you first, and you know I can. If you want to live, don't sleep tonight. If you do, it'll be the last night you sleep on this earth."

"You…you can't do that."

"I can, and I will."

"You're talking nonsense," he screamed.

"Can you take the chance? Sleep and you die. Tonight," she said in a low, menacing tone of voice. The boy ran out of the room and into the long hallway. "How unfortunate you're such a dull child!" she yelled at the fleeing body.

# CHAPTER 104

Nadine arrived in the dining room promptly at nine o'clock. An attaché directed her to the proper chair at the table where she was to be seated and reminded her to remain standing until the ambassador arrived. The children arrived and stood behind their chairs opposite Nadine. A few minutes later, the Chens arrived taking their respective positions at the opposite ends of the table. A formally attired young man entered the dining room carrying a soup tureen.

Once everyone was served, Nadine turned to the ambassador and said, "It has come to my attention that evening meals are served at nine o'clock." Without waiting for the ambassador to reply, she continued. "That is too late for children of their age to be eating. Henceforth, the children and I will be dining upstairs in the spare room at six o'clock. Please notify those in charge to prepare the room for tomorrow evening's meal." The ambassador nodded his head in agreement.

"Also," Nadine continued, "children should not be allowed to select their bedtime.  Henceforth, both children must be bathed, dressed for bed, and in bed no later than eight o'clock."

"That's whack," the boy bellowed.  He threw back his chair and started to run around the table to attack Nadine who sat calmly ladling a spoonful of soup into her mouth when the boy heard his father command in Chinese, "Sit down!"  The boy slowly retreated to his chair, folded his arms in protest, and refused to eat.  The ambassador turned to Nadine and said quietly in English, "All that you ask shall be done."

The boy jumped out of his chair and ran from the dining room.  Moments later, Nadine excused herself from the table and went to the boy's room.  She knocked softly on the door.  When there was no answer, she opened it and entered the room where she found the boy on the bed sniffling sniffles of rage.  She stood close to the bed, looked down at him, and in a hateful tone of voice said, "How unfortunate you're such a dull child."  That said, she left the room and rejoined the ambassador, his wife, and the little girl for a pleasurable, quiet meal.

# CHAPTER 105

Nadine was first to arrive in the dining room at seven the next morning. A few minutes later the girl arrived followed by the Chens. The ambassador motioned to one of the servers and whispered something in his ear. The young man left the room on the run. Minutes later the boy stumbled into the dining room in his pajamas, hair uncombed, looking haggard as if he hadn't slept.

The ambassador took one look at the boy and commanded him to return to his room and make himself presentable. The ambassador told the boy in Chinese he had five minutes to do so. "Now run!" he demanded. The boy ran out of the dining room. Much to Nadine's surprise, the ambassador looked in her direction and nodded his head slightly.

Minutes later the boy returned to the dining room looking presentable. Nadine thought she saw an ever so slight look of satisfaction spread across the ambassador's face that the boy had obeyed his father's commands.

Nadine continued eating her breakfast until she decided the moment was right to introduce the next item on her agenda. "Boy," she said in a loud voice looking across the table at the boy. "Look at me when I speak to you." Slowly the boy raised his head and looked at Nadine.

"When any door is closed, especially a lady's door, always knock before entering. Never enter a room without permission. Do you understand me, boy?" she said in a derisive tone of voice.

The boy nodded his head *yes*.

In the same derisive voice as before, Nadine responded with, "I doubt it. How unfortunate you're such a dull child!"

Ambassador Chen remained silent. Mrs. Chen's facial expression was one of horror that her son was being disrespected by a foreign woman. Nadine realized she had just made a dangerous enemy. She knew this was a problem that had to be solved if she was to remain in the Chen household and fulfill her mission.

# CHAPTER 106

The next three days passed quietly. Nadine and the two children had their evening meal served at six o'clock in the spare room that had been made into a charming place in which to dine. The children were bathed, dressed for bed, and in bed by eight. The boy, no longer fearing for his life as he slept, regained his normal appearance of good health.

On the fourth day, Nadine called the children into the spare room for a *little talk* as she called it. She informed both children they were to say separately to each parent in Chinese the following: 'Dearest Father or Dearest Mother: I humbly apologize for the nasty things I have said to you. I humbly apologize for the way I have acted. I know I have not shown you proper respect. Please forgive me because I love you very much, and I cannot live without your love.'

"I've written it down for you in English. You are to go to your rooms and practice saying these words in Chinese until every word you utter is said with the proper emotion, conviction, and sincerity. You have one day to learn this. Tomorrow evening after the six o'clock meal, I will listen to each of you say it in Chinese. Because I do not understand Chinese, your words, your facial expressions must convey the meaning of each word so that I can feel the emotion of each word spoken. If I am satisfied you have mastered these words, the next morning after breakfast, each of you will go separately into your father's study and tell him you have something important to say to him. Then you will say these words." She looked at the boy and said, "Boy! Do you think you can remember all these words?"

The boy nodded his head *yes*.

"I doubt it," Nadine sneered. "How unfortunate you're such a dull child."

# CHAPTER 107

Nadine heard the children recite the words she had written for them after the six o'clock meal the next evening. She hadn't expected them to remember the words let alone convey any meaning to them. Much to her surprise, both had taken the assignment seriously, and as they recited the words, their facial expressions, the emotion in their voices, but most of all their moist eyes revealed an inner-most desire and need to be loved.

The next morning just as the ambassador was finishing his breakfast, Nadine turned to him and said, "If you could spare a few moments after breakfast this morning, the children would like to speak to you privately in your study."

"I suppose so," the ambassador said gruffly, "but they'll have to make it snappy." Nadine could tell the word *snappy* pleased him because it demonstrated his knowledge of English idioms. "I have several important people coming this morning, and I don't want my children interfering in the proceedings. Is that understood?"

"Perfectly," Nadine said unflinchingly. "Please notify the children when you are ready."

The ambassador finished his tea, looked at his watch, and said unenthusiastically, "I suppose now is as good a time as any." He stood and left the dining room.

The ambassador entered the study. He left the door open and seated himself behind a large mahogany desk. The boy quietly knocked on the opened study door. "Come in, come in. I don't have all day," the ambassador said gruffly focusing his attention on the papers in front of him.

The boy slowly closed the study door. The girl fidgeted, waiting her turn. Many nervous minutes passed. She could stand it no longer. She knocked on the door. Permission to enter was slow in coming, but when it did, she carefully turned the huge doorknob with her small hand. The door unlatched and she moved it forward just enough so she could squeeze her tiny body through the small opening. Then she closed it ever-so-slowly behind her.

Nadine waited in the adjoining hallway where she was joined by three well-dressed men whom she supposed were American businessmen by their appearance. When the study door finally opened, it was obvious something miraculous had taken place inside the once imposing study's four walls.

# CHAPTER 108

In an unemotional voice, Nadine said to the children, "Your father is a very busy man, and he must see these gentlemen." She moved toward the children to take them away from their father, but it was obvious the ambassador didn't want to let go of his children, nor did they want to leave his loving arms.

The ambassador finally released his firm hold and asked his children, "May I have a kiss?" He bent down and as he did so, the children kissed their father on the lips and put their arms around his neck hugging him lovingly. When they finally let go, he stood to his full height and whispered in English, "How about lunch at McDonald's today?"

"Can we, can we?" the children squealed in delight because never before had they been allowed inside a McDonald's let alone eat there.

"We can, and we will. Twelve noon today," the ambassador said gleefully.

"All right, children," Nadine prompted. "You have more work to do. Wave good-bye to your father." In a firm voice, she said, "Follow me." Seconds later they arrived at their mother's door. She nodded to the boy who knew what he must do. He knocked quietly. A pleasant voice on the other side answered in Chinese, "Please come in."

The boy disappeared behind the closed door. Minutes passed until the boy opened the door so his sister could enter. He closed the door behind her and waited with Nadine in the hallway. She couldn't help but notice his emotional state with his sniffling every few seconds. Moments later, Mrs. Chen, hand-in-hand with her young daughter, opened the door. Both were in tears. The boy ran to his mother who embraced her children kissing them repeatedly on their cheeks and lips.

When the moment had passed, the girl looked up at her mother and said, "You'll never guess where daddy is taking us for lunch today." Before her mother could respond, she screamed, "McDonald's." Then she added, "Please come too. Please."

The boy looked at his mother with tears in his eyes and said, "Please come."

Through a new veil of tears, Mrs. Chen in flowery Chinese assured her children she would be most honored to accompany her most wonderful children to the most venerable establishment called McDonald's.  Both children yelled in delight kissing their mother many more times.

When things settled down, Mrs. Chen turned to Nadine and in English said, "Thank you for your most precious gift: the love of my children."

# CHAPTER 109

During the next few days, the children recited their apologies to the staff-members working in the home and to those who entered the Chen household whether on official business or as tradespeople. Nadine felt both children overacted when they saw the positive effect their apologies had on those to whom they apologized. It became obvious they came to enjoy their little apologetic performances and were disappointed when there was no one left to apologize to.

In the months that followed, the Chen household settled down to a loving atmosphere. Nevertheless, Nadine never stopped reminding the boy how unfortunate he was such a dull child. The boy resented her admonitions even though she had reunited him with his parents' love something he valued more and more as each day passed as he came to realize the tremendous pressures under which his father labored.

The children had just completed their studies one warm afternoon when the boy knocked feverishly on Nadine's door to inform her of the astonishing news he had just heard. Breathlessly, he told her some rich, important people had been arrested for buying stolen jewelry.

"The jewelry's been missing for a long, long time, and no one knows where it's been all this time," the boy said, enjoying the importance of his news. "I wonder who stole all that stuff, and where he kept it all." Then he turned to Nadine and said with great respect, "I sure would like to meet him."

The boy switched on the TV so Nadine could see the arrested people. There they were: her associates: Judge Alice Morrison; Canadian Prime Minister Thackery O'Connell and his wife Sylvia; Jeremy Heagle: the Toffee King; Cardinal Giuseppe DiVinci: Director of the Vatican Bank; Anita Pierson: Purdue feminist professor; Matthew Luke John: TV Evangelist; Theodora Friedenberg: Dutch novelist and Chairwoman of the EU Financial Board; Hans Stager: Swiss Bank President; and Sassy Fras: loud-mouthed, vulgar actress: arrested on suspicion of buying and possessing Jewish owned, Nazi stolen jewelry.

Now Nadine understood why her associates wanted their baubles back so badly, why they hadn't put them in a bank vault for fear of being discovered, and why they refused to file for the insurance money. It had never been about the money. They knew such a claim would expose their criminality.

Nadine was pleased she had stolen the jewels and even more pleased their liberation was doing the work no one had been able to accomplish since the fall of the Nazis: to bring at least a few criminals to justice. She settled back in the chair and watched her once proud and haughty associates hide their faces from the press and an aroused public.

# CHAPTER 110

Many months had passed since the Chen children's apology tour. Despite the new-found love between parents and children, forces from outside the ambassador's home in the form of important looking men in business suits and military uniforms threatened the tranquility of the Chen household. With so many Chinese officials coming and going at all hours of the day and night, Nadine realized something important was in the planning stages.

One frosty Monday in early January, she and the children had finished the evening meal. She had just returned to her room when she heard a soft knock on the door. "Come in," she said gently. The door opened. The boy entered the room smiling, making certain to close the door behind him. "What makes you so happy this evening?" she inquired.

"Things. Things you wouldn't understand," the boy said in a snotty tone of voice.

"You're probably right.  Now that you've said your little speech, you can leave."

The boy stood his ground.  "I'm tired of you calling me a dull child."

"I wouldn't say it if it wasn't true."

"What if I proved to you I wasn't a dull child.  Would you stop saying that to me?"

"Oh no you don't.  I don't make promises to dull children who have nothing important to say."

"What if I did have something important to say?"

"Oh, all right.  Stop teasing me with your nonsense.  Say what you have to say and go to bed."

"You know all those men who come into house?"

"They would be hard to miss."

"Have you ever heard of Taiwan?"

"Who hasn't?"

"What if I told you we're planning to invade Taiwan?"

"That's old news.  China's been threatening to do that for as many years as I can remember."

"You know those islands we built in the East and South China Seas?"

"Who doesn't?"

"Right at this moment, we're building up our forces on those islands not just to invade Taiwan but The Philippines and Japan too," he boasted. "Huge war coming."

"What jibber-jabbish you're talking. Pure nonsense. You think you can fool your nanny into not calling you a dull child with such nonsense?"

"It's not nonsense," the boy said adamantly. "Want to know something else?"

"No thank you. I think you've been watching too many violent movies."

"We've been building underground tunnels in North Korea. Our soldiers are there now. Soon they'll invade South Korea while our ally, the Iranians, will destroy Israel with missiles and atomic bombs. All at the same time," he added breathlessly.

"How could you possibly know about such things."

"My father lets me listen to the talks with the generals. He says he's preparing me for the diplomatic service and that I should learn about these things at an early age."

"And when is all this to take place?"

"The third of June. You wait and see if it doesn't happen. I bet you won't call me a dull child when we've invaded all those places."

"I'll believe it when I see it," Nadine said in a derisive voice. "Now it's time for a dull child to go to bed. Now!" she scowled.

# CHAPTER 111

Nadine seldom left the embassy, and when she did, she only went on her days off, Thursdays and Sundays, to take a brisk walk in Central Park. It was these Central Park visits that gave her the opportunity to pass and receive messages. A different agent, sometimes male, sometimes female, would attract her attention in any variety of ways to make it appear like two strangers passing in the park. Once contact was made, the agent would quietly say the word *Chameleon.* When Nadine nodded in the affirmative or smiled, the agent went on his or her way meeting other agents posing as friends, wives, boyfriends, girlfriends, whatever cover Perky concocted for them.

Nadine would then continue to walk around the park, stopping occasionally to enjoy the sights and sounds the park had to offer. After a few minutes of brisk walking, she would purchase a vitamin water from a vendor that she delicately sipped through a straw, slip her coded message into the folded napkin that she wrapped around the base of the bottle, take a few more sips of the water, and place the bottle and napkin into a different trash can each time. She would walk a bit more and then exit the park.

FBI agents carefully watched the trash can to be certain no one removed it. They let it sit seemingly unattended for hours until an agent drove up in a motorized cart and took it to a special garage where the bottle and napkin were separated from the rest of the trash.

Even though Nadine placed her bottle of vitamin water and napkin in a different trash can each time, Chinese undercover agents became suspicious of a repeated action over a period of months. One of the Chinese undercover agents reached into a trash can to search for the bottle of vitamin water when an in-line skater plowed into him at such a high rate of speed that it sent him sprawling to the sidewalk. The unconscious agent was taken to a hospital with a severe concussion. Another agent tried to retrieve a bottle when a pit bull somehow got lose from its owner and bit the agent so severely he had to be rushed to a hospital for immediate surgery. After these two unforeseeable incidents, no Chinese agent went near any trash can in the park.

# CHAPTER 112

The boy told Nadine of the Chinese invasion plans on a Monday evening. She had given her report the previous day that stated she had nothing new to report except she continued the strategy of calling the boy a most dull child in hopes he might disclose important information. Now that the strategy had worked, it was imperative she convey what she had learned as quickly as possible. She realized a second visit to the park in the same week was risky, but she had to chance it. She knew Perky wouldn't be expecting her, but maybe, just maybe, there might be an agent in the park.

Thursday was an unusually beautiful January day filled with sunshine and temperatures well up in the sixties. Nadine persuaded the children's teacher to let the children have an extra hour for lunch so she could take them to the park and enjoy the unusually warm day outdoors.

Central Park was crowded with thousands of New Yorkers celebrating the warm day with T-shirts, shorts, and sandals. The usual cast of skaters and cyclists along with shirtless young men showing off their various soccer moves were all present as well as street magicians who captivated the children's attention while Nadine searched the crowd for an agent. She looked in all directions until she saw a hopeful sign: a woman reading a magazine that featured on its cover a chameleon perched on a branch with the tag line, *New York Is Changing,* each letter in the tag line a different color. Nadine smiled and returned to the children.

She tapped the mesmerized children on the shoulder and informed them the hour was nearly up. "We don't want to make teacher angry, do we?" Nadine asked in a pleasant tone of voice.

"No!" the children shouted back playfully.

"Before we leave, would you like an ice cream or something to drink?" The children voted for ice cream.

Nadine took them to a park vendor and bought chocolate ice cream cones for each and a bottle of vitamin water for herself around which she wrapped a napkin with the coded message. "Why do you always drink that icky vitamin water?" the boy asked shuddering at the memory when he had tried it. "That stuff is nasty. I don't know how you drink it."

Nadine laughed as she took several more sips through the straw and said, "All right. I won't drink any more of it." She placed the napkin wrapped bottle in the trash can and ushered the children from the park. She told them they must hurry so as not to take advantage of their teacher's generosity in giving them an extra hour for lunch. She also admonished them not to mention the ice cream cones although she knew that was an impossible task since both children had dripped chocolate on their shirts.

# CHAPTER 113

Nadine hoped the Thursday message had been received and the proper military authorities alerted, but there was no way to know. The remainder of January and the months of February and March were cold and snowy in New York making it impossible to establish contact with agents in the park. She listened to news broadcasts, but there was no mention of a Chinese military build-up on the island bases or even a hint of China's intentions to invade the Pacific Rim nations. The world seemed peaceful.

Nadine's world was anything but peaceful. Her mission was accomplished. It was time to leave, but without orders from Perky, she had to stay where she was. She feared for her safety. Her fear centered on one person: the dull child. If he accidentally let slip or intentionally bragged to his father that he told her about the invasion plans, the ambassador would inform the Chinese secret service who would throw her in a dark hole and starve her to death.  Surprisingly, the thought of being shot or even hanged brought relief.  *At least it'll be quick,* the mind reasoned.

Another thought staved off panic.  The boy hadn't said a word to his father about informing her of the invasion.  Either he didn't think his telling her was important or he knew he would be in serious trouble if he mentioned it to his father.  Nadine's fate lay in the hands of a most dull child, and she didn't like it.

# CHAPTER 114

News of a different kind dominated the media during those endless winter months: the trials of Nadine's associates. Jewish families, who for many decades claimed the Nazis had stolen their families' jewelry, described and drew replicas of the jewelry in question. It had been painstaking work, but the jewels some of these families described were found to have been in the possession of the associates.

The associates' trials were short in duration because there was no defending the indefensible. Tried separately in different parts of the world, all were convicted of knowingly buying and possessing Jewish owned, Nazi stolen jewelry. Nadine watched as pale-faced, tearful, and in some cases hysterical associates were escorted from courtrooms by burly policemen to begin long prison sentences for their crimes. Through her appropriations of the rich and arrogant, Nadine had partially solved an old crime, had reunited a few families with their possessions, and brought to justice those who had engaged in the possession of stolen goods. *Well done, Nadine*, she congratulated herself.

# CHAPTER 115

Nadine anxiously awaited the first Thursday or Sunday when the weather would permit her to visit Central Park and hopefully establish contact with one of Perky's agents. That day was a long time in coming as winter snows turned to spring rains. On a Sunday in early May, the clouds parted, and the temperature rose into the mid-seventies. Nadine reveled in the sunshine and its warmth as she walked slowly through the park in search of a contact. Much to her dismay, she saw no one.

Her time in the park was coming to an end when she heard a woman screaming, "Help! Help! Those hoodlums tried to rape me. Someone call 911." Nadine saw a group of men wearing ski masks running toward her. Suddenly, her world spun out of control as the men threw her to the ground, crowded around her spread-eagled body, and chanted, "Fuck her! Fuck her!"

Flat on her back, she looked into the dark eyes of a man hunched over her. As he ripped her clothes, he asked quietly, "Chameleon?" Shaken by the suddenness of the attack, she didn't answer. The man asked again, "Chameleon?" whereupon she nodded her head *yes*.

The man jumped on top of her and tore her light sweater while another man pulled down her jeans. She felt the man on top of her shove something under her left breast. "Gift from Perky," followed by the words, "No sound," then in an unfriendly voice say, "Stay put!" He slapped her hard across the mouth and punched her in the left eye. He yelled above the roar of the others, "*Otra puta blanca chingada.*" A member of the group proudly declared to the gawking by-standers, "Another white bitch fucked. Let that be a warning to all yous white bitches. You ain't safe nowheres," followed by cheers from the others who kicked her repeatedly. The man pulled up his pants while the others roared with laughter. In an instant, they were gone.

Nadine lay on the ground. Several women helped her to her feet screaming in disgust, "The park's no safe. Where are the *policias* when we need them!"

# CHAPTER 116

Nadine limped out of the park to the embassy where she pushed the buzzer to gain entrance. When the attaché opened the door, he was shocked to see her in such an unkempt condition. "I'm all right," she assured him as she entered the embassy. "I'll just go to my room. Please don't tell anyone about this."

"I'm sorry, Miss Dalton. I have no choice in the matter. An attack against any staff-member is an attack against the embassy and the Chinese people. I must report this incident to the ambassador immediately."

"All right, all right," she muttered in a weak voice as she limped down the long hallway toward the steep staircase. "Do as you must. I'll be in my room."

Once in the privacy of her room, she reached under her left breast. She smiled as her hand grasped the key: the key that had made her a fortune: the key that had incarcerated twenty-two associates.  Just as she was ready to remove it from its private place, she heard a soft knock.  "Come in," she said in a strong voice meant to convey that all was well.

The ambassador rushed into the room in uncharacteristic haste.  One look at Nadine prompted him to blurt, "I was right to call a doctor: an American doctor.  I thought you'd feel more comfortable with an American.  He'll be here in a few minutes."  In a voice filled with concern, he asked, "Who attacked you?  I assure you your attackers will be caught and brought to justice.  Such an attack is an attack against the Chinese people."  His words conveyed his official position, but the worry in his eyes conveyed his deepest most personal feelings.  The mind realized she was his secret love as he took her hand in a spontaneous, affectionate gesture that surprised him as well as her.

Her hand in his, the mind laughed at the thought that men regardless of how rugged their outward appearance or how forceful their words, underneath that façade, whether they be American, French, Russian, or Chinese, they were all the same: like a prickly pear: prickly on the outside and soft on the inside.

# CHAPTER 117

The ambassador, holding Nadine's hand, fussed over her. Tired of his presence, she asked if she could have a few minutes to freshen up before the doctor arrived. The ambassador apologized for having intruded at such a difficult time and walked slowly toward the door. As he placed his hand on the door's side and began to close it, he stopped and turned to face her. "I care what happens to you." These few words, spoken with great emotion, expressed his innermost feelings. He waited for a response. When none came, he added, "Someone who can return my children's love is worth saving." With that, he closed the door behind him.

Nadine scanned the room looking for a place to hide the key. She started to reach for it beneath her breast when she heard a loud knock on the door. "Come in," she said pleasantly expecting the doctor. The boy flung open the door relishing in the fact his nemesis had suffered significant injuries and in a snotty, sarcastic voice said, "You're such a dull woman." His message delivered, he slammed the door shut.

Nadine lost no time in hiding the key. She carefully removed the two-way tape that encircled it and placed the magnetized key under the metal bed brace. She barely had time to stand upright when she heard a knock at the door. "Please come in," she said gently, relieved to see a gray-haired man carrying a black physician's bag.

After a brief examination, the doctor informed Nadine and a greatly relieved ambassador that the worst injuries she had sustained were nothing more than scrapes and bruises with a good possibility of a black, left eye.

# CHAPTER 118

The black eye became a reality: a development that brought great joy to the boy and girl. Their father warned them not to make fun of their nanny's condition: a warning they gleefully disobeyed. Nadine might have brought love and tranquility to the Chen family, but as far as she and the children were concerned, no such events had occurred.

Once Nadine's injuries became old news, the parade of visitors in and out of her room ceased. Without disruptions, the mind could focus on recent events and their significance. Paramount in the mind was why had Perky returned the key? Nadine never expected to see it again let alone be reunited with it.

After much consideration, the mind came up with an unsettling answer. Perky was in trouble: money trouble stemming from the confiscation of the Caliphate's funds. If he were in trouble that meant she was too. The fake rape with its physical injuries and the words *stay put* was his way of telling her she was safe from prosecution as long as she stayed in the embassy.

The key was another matter altogether.  Did its return signify her contact with Perky and Jocko ceased to exist: that she was a free woman who could once again ply her trade as an appropriator?  That was a liberating thought but one that was overshadowed by the reality she couldn't leave the embassy. She had no money and nowhere to go, but if she remained in the embassy, she could be exposed as a spy.

# CHAPTER 119

The mind replayed the rape repeatedly. One thing it couldn't make sense of was the two words *no sound*. What did those two words mean? The obvious meaning was she shouldn't scream, but if the would-be rapist didn't want her to scream, why didn't he say, "Don't scream?" He could have just as easily covered her mouth with his hand to stifle her screams, but he didn't. In fact, he should have wanted her to scream which would have been perfectly normal in such a setting, but he didn't. There had to be more to those two words than a warning for her not to scream. Tired of trying to decipher any additional meaning, the mind turned to words she understood: the ambassador's last words before he left her room: *someone who can return my children's love is worth saving.*

The mind carefully parsed the meanings of the word *saving.* Did the ambassador mean *saving* as in keeping her in his employ since she had solved his children problem, or did he mean he was *saving* her from being identified as a park-rape-victim and the attendant publicity?  There was a third meaning of *saving* that concerned her the most: that he knew she was a spy and for his own sexual fantasies decided she was worth *saving* from a death-sentence?

The mind realized the last meaning was ridiculous. Why would the ambassador of a powerful nation betray his country at such an important historical moment for a woman with whom his closest sexual contact had been to hold her hand for a few moments?  The mind decided it was a combination of the first two meanings: that she was a good nanny and the ambassador was saving her from unwanted publicity since that would reflect badly on himself and the embassy. Nevertheless, the mind couldn't let go the possibility that the ambassador knew her deepest secret: that she was the one who had betrayed him.  Her life now depended on not just the dull child but the ambassador as well.

# CHAPTER 120

Activity in the residence became frenetic. One unsettling aspect of the ceaseless activity was the ambassador hadn't spoken to Nadine since he left her room after the park-attack. The mind attempted to dismiss this lack of communication as nothing more than the ambassador being too busy to talk to his children's nanny, yet it feared this isolation could mean something far more significant. It reasoned that perhaps the ambassador was waiting until after the invasion to have her arrested to avoid an embarrassing situation at such an important moment in his political career.

One evening after dinner, Nadine flicked on the television and there he was: Maurice Pangle, Director of the FBI, expressing outrage that one of his agents had gone rogue and in so doing had not only seriously damaged the reputation of the FBI but had also endangered the safety of the nation. "Without my personal authorization," Pangle fumed, "a rogue agent conducted a sting operation against members of the Caliphate whose sole aim is to enable Moslems to have a state of their own in which they can pursue the tenets of the true Moslem religion.

"This agent," Pangle continued, "not only had the temerity to engage in this illegal operation but stole the organization's money and used it for his own personal use. The photo you are now witnessing is that of Bud Perkins who has been arrested and incarcerated. However, this agent was not alone in this illegal operation. With permission of the CIA Director, Lazlo Lothar, I can now reveal the surprising identity of Perkin's CIA accomplice, a man who has been using one name for decades, Jocko, but whose real name is Giacomo Gianni. He has also been arrested and incarcerated." An unflattering picture of Jocko appeared.

"These two men were not alone in this perfidious act against the Caliphate. They employed a female agent who has not as yet been apprehended. If you have any information about this woman," a sketch of Nadine appeared, "contact your nearest FBI office immediately so this individual can be apprehended and incarcerated."

Nadine was pleased the drawing bore no resemblance to her. The only part that was accurate was the red wig. That was reassuring, but the loss of Perky and Jocko greatly concerned her. Without them, her future was very much in doubt.

# CHAPTER 121

A world that only a short time ago seemed peaceful suddenly erupted into chaos. The arrests of Perky and Jocko were just the beginning. Two days after their arrest, three spies reputedly linked to the Russian government were arrested in London for attempting to crash the British and American economies. Several days later, the evening news was filled with shocking revelations of international child prostitution and drug smuggling networks. Photos of the three Russians from the Bright Spot Diner appeared identified as the kingpins of the murderous drug and prostitution operations.

Then all hell broke loose. The date was May 31. It was a little after seven in the morning. Nadine had just gotten up and dressed when suddenly the boy threw open the door and ran into the room with the most shocking news: news that would not just shock the world but rock it.

# CHAPTER 122

"**B**ombs...bombs...YOU!" the boy screamed in anguish. He turned and ran from the room yelling in Chinese, "No die, no die" as he fled down the long hallway.

Nadine rushed to the TV and switched it on. Scenes of massive destruction filled the screen with a reporter's voice in the background trying to describe developing events. "It's too early to determine whether nuclear devices have been detonated," the frightened reporter spoke in an excited voice, "but it is certain the Americans have attacked the man-made islands built by the Chinese in both the East and South China Seas and numerous North Korean installations while Israeli jets destroyed the Iranian air force, missile sites, and government buildings in Tehran."

Nadine clicked off the TV and slumped back in the chair. She knew sooner or later the Chinese secret service would investigate every person in the embassy, and she, being an American, would fall under immediate suspicion. She waited patiently to be questioned or worse yet: arrested. While she waited, the mind kicked into action without any coaxing. It focused on the word *you.* When the boy said *you,* did he mean her personally, or did he mean Americans and Israelis? Nadine smiled. What difference did it make? Her days as a spy had come to an end.

The attaché standing in the open doorway said softly, "Miss Dalton?" When he had her attention, he said in a barely audible voice, "No one is to enter or leave the residence without permission." Nadine nodded her head she understood. The attaché left as quietly as he had appeared.

Alone in her room, Nadine needed to believe she was a heroine saving millions of lives by having millions killed, a troubling inconsistency, but this was no time to philosophize about moral issues when her personal safety was at stake. She was a victim of her own making. She had snapped the trap shut. Now she was caught in it.

# CHAPTER 123

An eerie stillness descended upon the embassy. Nadine stayed in her room. The ambassador confined himself to his study, Mrs. Chen remained in her bedroom, and the once vivacious children became sullen trying to amuse themselves by playing video games and watching cartoons on their I-pads but to no avail. Nothing could cheer them up. Meals were eaten in silence with each of them staring blankly at their plates eating only because it was a necessity.

In early July, a bombshell of a different kind happened in Russia. The UN declared Vetrov, President of Russia, a criminal for his leadership in organizing and profiting from the international drug and sex trades and his plot to crash the British and American economies. The UN demanded his immediate arrest.

Soon after his crimes became public knowledge, angry crowds formed in Red Square. A number of high-level Russian army generals mutinied and demanded Vetrov's removal from office.  Furious, Vetrov called for the generals' arrest and execution, but as more and more generals defected, even his closest friends turned against him.

Angered by Vetrov's vicious enslavement of young girls for prostitution, soldiers encircled the Kremlin so no one could enter or leave. They searched every part of it looking for Vetrov but without success.  It was drunken soldiers who accidentally stumbled upon him cowering in a basement closet in nearby Saint Basil's Cathedral.  They fired numerous bullets into his body, urinated on the shattered remains, and dragged it from the cathedral to Red Square for all to see.  Once the viewing ended, they threw the body in the back of a rusty, old truck and took it to a farm north of Moscow where they cut it up into little pieces, mixed the remains with garbage, and fed it to the pigs.  Soldiers shouted at the snorting pigs as they devoured Vetrov's remains, "This is for all the innocent, young girls you killed, you pig."

# CHAPTER 124

Loud shouts from the downstairs hallway roused Nadine from a deep sleep. She glanced at the clock: 2:58 a.m. Instinctively, she reached under the bed brace and retrieved the key. She hastily wrapped the double-sided tape around the key and placed it under her left breast. Moments later, the door burst open. A man aimed a pistol at her head and demanded in English, "Dress now. I wait: outside." He left the room but didn't close the door.

Nadine quickly pulled blue-jeans and a sweater over her pajamas.

"Hurry!" the man demanded.

"I'm hurrying as fast as I can," she replied in an uncertain voice. She took a pair of socks from a dresser drawer, quickly put them on, and slipped into sneakers. Just as she bent over to tie them, the man said in a harsh voice, "Time over!" She grabbed a light jacket from the closet before he pushed her from the room, down the stairs to the hallway below where the household personnel, the attachés, and the Chen family were assembled.

When the ambassador saw Nadine, he cried out in Chinese, "No! You can't take her. She's an American citizen."

Another man punched him in the stomach: something no one would have dared do a few weeks previously. The man's anger told Nadine all she needed to know that the suspicion of guilt for the failure of the invasion had fallen on the ambassador.

Horrified at seeing their father so badly treated, the boy and the girl cried out, but the men told them to *shut up.* The ambassador tried to look strong to reassure his children he was all right, but the pain in his stomach was so severe he was unable to stand let alone speak to his children.

"Move!" one of the men commanded. He pointed his pistol to the rear of the house. It was then Nadine realized her fear of being shoved in a hole and starved to death was about to become a reality.

# CHAPTER 125

The flight took countless hours. The windowless plane made it impossible to look for landmarks. When it landed, Nadine realized she was probably somewhere in China. A windowless van drove her, the Chen family, and the embassy staff to an undisclosed location.

Nadine was escorted to a prison cell where she was instructed to strip and put on prison-regulation clothing that had been placed on a metal bed that also contained a well-used pillow and blanket. A slot at the bottom of the door opened. A tray was pushed through it that contained a small bowl of rice, an unwashed, raw carrot, and a cup of water. Nadine knew from experience she had to eat and drink everything that was offered no matter how revolting the food might be if she had the smallest chance of surviving this ordeal.

Hours later, the need to relieve herself became an issue. She looked about the room and located a small bucket tucked under the bed.  She didn't hesitate to use it.  As she squatted above the jagged edged bucket, she closed her eyes and pretended she was in the bathroom of a five-star hotel with marble floors and golden sinks.  When she opened her eyes, she had to face the grim reality of her surroundings.

# CHAPTER 126

"I know you are a spy," the interrogator began. "There is no denying it." He stared a long, intimating stare before he continued. "I know you had contacts in New York City's Central Park." He paused. "I know you passed military secrets to these contacts either by vitamin water bottles or the napkins wrapped around them." He paused. "These are all indisputable facts." He raised his hand to quiet Nadine even though she offered no response.

"The question to solve was this: how did you learn these secrets?" He paused. "We realized Ambassador Chen would never give you secrets. Then we discovered a most interesting piece of information. The ambassador allowed his ten-year-old son to attend military meetings." He paused. "We also know you called the boy *a most dull child.* Putting one and one together as you Americans say, we know the boy revealed secrets you passed to contacts in park."

The interrogator stood. "Follow me." Nadine followed him down a long, well-guarded hallway. He opened the door to a room in which there were four chairs facing forward. He turned to Nadine and said in a cold voice, "I must inform you I have received proper payment for this operation."

The interrogator barked an order in Chinese. A door opened. Mr. and Mrs. Chen entered. They stood face forward in front of the first two chairs.

"Sit!" the interrogator commanded in Chinese. The Chens sat down. The interrogator called for a soldier to enter the room. On command, he thrust the ambassador's head down and fired a shot into the back of it. The interrogator said coldly, "Wife no good without husband." The soldier thrust her neck down and fired a shot into the back of her head.

The interrogator barked another command. A soldier holding the hands of the boy and girl entered the room. He pushed them into the two remaining chairs. "Children no good without parents," the interrogator said without emotion. The soldier shot the boy and then the girl. The interrogator turned to Nadine and in a harsh voice said, "You see what we do with those who betray us. Come. Follow me."

# CHAPTER 127

Nadine followed the interrogator to a room across the hall from where the Chen family had been executed. The interrogator opened the door and motioned for Nadine to enter. She saw a single chair facing forward. "Sit!" the interrogator commanded. Nadine did as he demanded.

The interrogator barked a command. Someone entered the room. A hand thrust her head forward. She felt something whiz past her left ear and the sound of a shot. Tense moments passed. She felt a second shot pass close to her right ear and the sound of a gun being discharged.

"I have a third shot waiting, and this time it won't miss. You have choice. Work for us and spare life. Refuse to work for us and die in next five seconds. What is it to be?"

"Yes, I'll work for you."

"Good," the interrogator said as he motioned the shooter to leave the room.  "You may stand now.  Follow me."  He left the room followed at a distance by a badly shaken Nadine whose legs shook so badly she could barely walk.

# CHAPTER 128

The interrogator informed Nadine she would be based in New York City. Her mission was to infiltrate UN diplomats to uncover American Israeli defense weaknesses. The interrogator reminded her repeatedly that wherever she went, whatever she did, she would be watched and any move on her part to make contact with any law-enforcement-agency would be her death warrant.

The commercial flight landed in New York where she was met by the Chinese contact, a disappointingly unattractive man who smelled strongly of cigarette smoke. Nadine had another disappointment when the taxi pulled up in front of a sleazy midtown hotel. *The Chinese are cheap,* ran through the mind as she and the contact walked through the crowded lobby filled with predominantly Asian men and a few American women whose profession was obvious even to the innocent.

The contact took her to the assigned room.  He opened the door, entered the room, and motioned for her to follow. "We have adjoining rooms with adjoining door which will be locked.  Only I have key," he said, pointing to the adjoining door.  He closed the hallway door and said, "Special lock on door.  Don't try to open it.  If you do, you'll get a most dangerous electrical shock."  He turned and disappeared behind the closing adjoining room door.  She heard the click of the lock click into place: then quiet.

Alone, she surveyed the sparsely furnished room not wanting to sit in the sweat stained chair or on the bed for fear of bedbugs, although the mind laughed at her squeamishness after all she had been through.  The mind realized the Chinese put her in seedy surroundings because they considered her undependable and expendable.  To them, she was a betrayer: a whore.  They intended to use this whore to their advantage with as little investment as possible.

The mind so engaged Nadine didn't hear the soft knock at the door.  A second louder knock snapped her to attention. She moved toward the door afraid to touch the knob for fear of a nasty shock.  She stood quietly while the mind weighed its options.  It decided she was already in a lose-lose situation, so she had nothing to lose by opening the door.

Much to her surprise, when she touched the knob, there was no shock. The door opened. She expected to see the contact, but the opened door revealed an old, Chinese char- woman. "Chameleon?" the old woman asked in a whispered voice. Nadine nodded her head yes. The woman reached into an empty bucket in the undercarriage of the cleaning cart and handed her a crumpled paper bag. "Everything you need. Leave in thirty minutes. Get in car in front." These words spoken, the old woman hobbled down the hallway slowly pushing the squeaking cleaning cart toward the elevator.

Nadine closed the door and examined the contents of the bag in which she found a slinky red dress slit up the side, red platform shoes, a blonde wig, a black jacket, and cheap cosmetics. She grasped the meaning of the bag's contents. She quickly went to work transforming herself into a worldly woman of the streets.

When she guessed the half hour had passed, she tossed the black jacket over her left shoulder and with long, leggy strides strode through the lobby garnering many lecherous looks from male on-lookers and pushed through the hotel's doors to the waiting car parked in front. Once in the car, the driver asked, "Chameleon?" When she said *yes*, the car sped away.

An hour later the car entered a private aviation hangar at Kennedy Airport.  A well-dressed man opened the door and asked, "Chameleon?"  When she said *yes,* he instructed her to follow him.  He motioned to a changing room where she found clothes more suitable for travel.  When she exited the changing room, the man laughed and asked softly, "Is that you, Chameleon?"  Nadine smiled and answered *yes.*  A few minutes later she found herself on board a private jet bound for an unknown destination.

# CHAPTER 129

Nadine awoke to a sunlit room. As she looked about her new surroundings, she could readily see it oozed with quaintness: the old-fashioned print wallpaper, the thick pillared oak bed posts, the hand-stitched quilt, the well-worn wood-plank floors, the blackened stones that encased the fireplace, all relics belonging to a time long past. She stretched and luxuriated in a room that its very being made her feel safe and secure.

She heard a soft knock at the door. "Come in," she said politely. A young woman dressed in a maid's uniform entered the room carrying a tray. "It's a little past four, Mum. It's teatime. I wasn't certain you'd be awake, but I took the liberty to prepare a small tray with hot tea and sandwiches in case you were."

Nadine sat upright in the bed and motioned for the maid to set the tray over her legs. As the maid prepared the tea to Nadine's liking, she asked the maid where she was. "All I can say about that, Mum, is you're in England, but you could tell that yourself by my accent. I hope you enjoy your tea and sandwiches, Mum. I'll return in a bit to collect the tray."

Nadine did as the maid suggested. She enjoyed her tea along with the sandwiches. Soon thereafter, she drifted into blissful sleep.

# CHAPTER 130

Nadine spent the next two weeks resting and walking about the gardens that adjoined the house. She had no idea where she was, and she didn't want to know. She knew she was safe where she was as long as she didn't *drift away* as a security guard so gently put it.

One autumn afternoon as she strolled about the garden enjoying the crisp fresh air and the colorful fall foliage, a maid rushed from the main house to inform her she was wanted in the library *immejiately*. *Finally, I meet my captors,* Nadine thought to herself.

# CHAPTER 131

When Nadine entered the library, a gentleman who had been quietly smoking his pipe awaiting her arrival quickly put it in a large ashtray specifically designed for just such an occasion. He stood to greet her with his out-stretched hand. Nadine walked briskly across the room to embrace it. The gentleman bowed slightly and motioned for her to sit in a chair near his.

Both seated, the gentleman picked up his pipe. He pointed its stem toward himself and said, "Permit me to introduce myself. I'm Sir Roger Fitz-Alan. No need to apologize for not recognizing me because we've never met." He waited for Nadine to say something. When she didn't, he continued. "For the last several years, you have been employed, for the lack of a better term, by two men known to you as Perky and Jocko."

Nadine nodded in the affirmative.

"The big question is: where does an Englishman fit into all this?  The answer is quite simple really.  Over the years, I have had the pleasure of working with both the American FBI and CIA.  As head of MI6, I do this quite frequently.  I think that pretty much sums up who I am and how I fit into the picture.

"Now to you," he said pointing the pipe's stem toward her.  "Of course, you realize you *have* been a bit of a bother," he said in such a charming manner that it had its desired effect on Nadine.  She felt comfortable in his presence.

"I didn't mean to be," she replied in a coquettish manner.

Sir Roger smiled his grandfatherly smile and replied, "I'm sure you didn't."  He reached into his pocket and pulled out a lighter, flicked it to flame, and lit his pipe.  "Wife says I should stop smoking, doctor says the same, and I agree with both, but…" he shrugged his shoulders, "I persist."  He snuggled back in the chair and contentedly puffed on a pipe that emitted wisps of grayish smoke with each puff.

After several more puffs, he held the lit pipe in his right hand and said quietly, "I'm quite certain you remember the night in Kansas City when you were arrested.  A night you more than likely would like to forget."

Nadine nodded her head *yes*.

"Yes, I thought you would, and I can't say as I blame you." He examined the tobacco in his pipe that had managed to extinguish itself. "It appears Perky must have gotten hold of your snaps," he said in an absent-minded manner more interested in the tobacco in his unlit pipe than the snaps.

"I came to that same conclusion some time ago. Either he got the photo from my high school yearbook or from a tape taken during a police raid at a locksmith's shop in Chicago. I'm not certain which."

"Chicago police raid. Jolly good. I say, you have led a rather interesting life," Sir Roger responded enthusiastically as he concluded the examination of the pipe tobacco. "Just as I thought. Tobacco packed too tightly. I have a habit of doing that, putting too much tobacco in the bowl trying to save time by not having to refill it so often." He took a small knife from his pocket and began to loosen the tobacco as he spoke. "Perky informed me he used your snap as a means of providing photo identification that he released to American airport security agencies. I imagine he felt he couldn't trust us foreigners with such a vital piece of information. He also informed me photo identification was the only way I would be able to make contact with you. Lucky for you, the flight from China arrived in New

York. Had it been Berlin, Paris, or even London I wouldn't have been able to help you."

Nadine smiled her appreciation.

"Now to skip forward to the recent past. When Perky and Jocko realized they were going to be arrested, they contacted me. They feared not for their own personal safety but yours. They specifically asked me to watch over you in case you got into serious trouble, which, as we both know, you did. The Chinese operation was a nasty bit of business from top to bottom, especially when the Chinese spirited you off to China. I was certain I had lost you. Nevertheless, just on the chance the inscrutable, unpredictable Chinese might do the predictable, I put American airport security on alert."

He reinserted the pipe in his mouth, flicked on the lighter, and relit the pipe. He smiled an indulgent smile pleased his pipe was drawing properly. After a few pleasing moments, he realized something was amiss. "Dash it. Pipe's out again. That's the trouble with a pipe. Always going out." He took the lighter out of his pocket and relit the pipe. He took several large puffs. Satisfied with the clouds of smoke after each puff, he continued. "As soon as you entered customs, Kennedy Airport security notified my office. I immediately sounded the alarm: *Chameleon has landed.* It was easy enough for agents to track your movements to the hotel. The hotel presented more troublesome problems."

He tapped the pipe tobacco with the heel of the lighter. He looked over the pipe at Nadine, smiled a sheepish smile, and said, "As you can see, pipe smoking is a full-time occupation. Where was I? Oh, yes, the hotel. Bad lot that. Den of thieves to put it politely. Of course, the Chinese watched your every move. That was to be expected.

"Damnable thing: a pipe. Never wants to stay lit. We'll give it a rest for now." He put it in the ashtray. "Fortunately the agent was able to disable the individuals who stood guard on your floor and the gentleman in the room adjoining yours. All the gentlemen were injected with a high-dosage anesthetic which will either give them a nice long rest or put them to rest permanently, depending on their physical condition, of course." He looked longingly at the pipe in the ashtray. He started to reach for it but thought better of it and retracted his hand in mid-air. "Most tempting that pipe. Oh, by the way, what did you think of the old Chinese charwoman who came to your room?"

"Surprise more than anything. I expected the man from the adjoining room."

"Never underestimate the charwoman, my dear Chameleon. She's the unsung heroine of many a spy novel as well as actual intelligence gathering. In your case, the old charwoman saved your life. Damn fine agent for one so young.

"Oh, speaking of agents, I have a bit of good news for you. Since you were never officially contracted by Perky, Jocko, or me personally, you have no obligation to continue service to the FBI, the CIA, or MI6. That means you are free to pursue your life as you wish." He looked into Nadine's eyes for a reaction to the news. There was none. *Damn well trained,* ran through Sir Roger's mind.

He paused as he rubbed his right hand over his forehead. "Let me see. What else did I have to tell you. Oh, yes. Almost forgot to mention this. The charwoman relieved the Chinese gentleman of something that might be of some interest to you. Perky made me promise if I ever had possession of this instrument, I was to return it to you. I know it works because it's how the charwoman not only blocked the electric mechanism attached to your hotel door but unlocked it as well."

He reached into his pocket, produced a key, and placed it in her hand. "Now that I've fulfilled my obligation to Perky, I must warn you. If you ever use this key or any other means in the taking of money, jewels, securities, or anything of value in the UK or any of its commonwealth nations, I shall personally see to it you never have another day of freedom. Do we understand each other?"

"We do," Nadine said without hesitation.

"Good. I'm glad that's settled. Oh, almost forgot. MI6 agents have deleted your photo identification data. Feel free to travel anywhere you want, although I wouldn't recommend a return trip to China just yet." He smiled at his little joke. When she remained expressionless, he concluded with, "All right, Chameleon. There's a chauffeur-driven car parked in front of the house. You're free as bird to go wherever you want." He stood, reinserted the pipe between his lips, shook her hand, and left the room.

Nadine carefully put the key in her pocket and followed Sir Roger's instruction. In less than five minutes, she was sitting in the back seat of a chauffeur driven Rolls headed for London.

# CHAPTER 132

Nadine's renewed freedom brought another worry as the Rolls sped along the motorway toward London. She was penniless. Perky had seized every cent she owned including her Swiss bank accounts. As the Rolls entered London's suburbs, she considered several options that would enable her to resume the extravagant, care-free lifestyle she had once enjoyed.

Lost in thought, she didn't hear the chauffeur softly say, "Mum?" He repeated it several times until she realized he was speaking to her. When he gained her attention, he handed her a business envelope. "Sir Roger asked me to give you this." Nadine opened the unsealed envelope. Inside was a letter neatly folded in thirds that read: *present this letter upon request* followed by Sir Roger's signature.

Thirty minutes later, the Rolls pulled up in front of the Bank of England. Sir William Walpole, Governor of the Bank, greeted her warmly when she presented him with Sir Roger's letter. Sir William then placed in her hand a ten-thousand-pound cashier's check expressing the gratitude of the British people for whom she had done so much. As Nadine walked out of Sir William's office not only did she feel ten-thousand-pounds richer but reborn, ready to re-embark on a satisfying, enriching life of appropriations.

# CHAPTER 133

Nadine reveled in the fact it was the head of the Bank of England and the British people who bankrolled her rebirth as an appropriator. *Quite appropriate,* she thought to herself, although she considered ten-thousand-pounds a paltry sum for what she had done. After all, she had saved the British Empire from financial destruction. *Something's better than nothing,* the mind reminded her.

A few weeks later, she invested most of the ten-thousand pounds in a dark-web-virtual-currency called Renewed Financial Resources, RFR, an innocuous name for a currency that was as powerful and accommodating as Crypto-Coin had been. Her life back in order, she wanted for nothing: except excitement. She loved planning and executing appropriations but limited to one a year left many days filled with nothing enriching to do, that is until the mind remembered Luis Sanchez's instruction in commodity trading.

Nadine plunged into her newfound interest with great enthusiasm. She soon discovered she had found the love of her life: the commodity markets. Their volatility with millions of dollars gained or lost in a matter of moments captured her emotions. Grains, gases, precious metals were all part of her commodity portfolio she manipulated with great skill providing many millions of dollars in profit.

Money had always been Nadine's main passion, but manipulation and control of others was a close second. She continued her mastery of sexual matters by breaking the hearts of many men and some women who cast their desires upon her without receiving anything in return. Several committed suicide which gave her even greater pleasure because it showed she had lost none of her charm or beauty as the years progressed.

One evening as she was thumbing through streaming video on her cell phone, she happened upon a program that was attempting to make a connection between the infamous robberies of the rich and famous from years ago with more recent robberies. The program's narrator made note of the fact that both robberies seemed to possess one important characteristic. "In both robberies," the narrator continued, "the most sophisticated security systems were deactivated allowing the thief or thieves to take whatever they desired.  However, in the first set of robberies, chimes sounded at eight-and ten-minute intervals that allowed police to link the robberies together. However, in this newest incantation of crimes, no such sounds can be heard."

Nadine jumped from the chair and screamed in delight, for at that moment, she understood what the mugger in the park meant when he said *no sound*.  Perky had added a new function to the key that blocked sound so the eight-and-ten-minute warnings couldn't be detected.  The thought had never occurred to her to ask the lock-shop owner to include the *no-sound* function. Now no law enforcement agency could link any of her appropriations together, and she had an FBI agent, Bud Perkins, as her partner in crime.  *Crime does pay,* she laughed to herself.

# CHAPTER 134

The world had changed, and Nadine had played a major role in changing it. Her only regret was she was unable to save the Chen family from execution. In her own way, she had become fond of the Chens: even the children, but she knew there was nothing she could have done to save them. She and the Chens were at the mercy of their captors. She also realized the Chens had outlived their usefulness. Their fate had to be execution. The only reason she had survived was her captors hoped she would be useful as a double agent.

She and Ambassador Chen had played the dangerous game of intelligence gathering. Surprisingly he, who had all the power, had lost. She, who had no power, had won, but she couldn't gloat at her victory. The sounds of bullets being fired into the heads of the Chens and the lifeless bodies of the boy and girl falling from the chairs onto the floor splattered with their parents' blood and brains were the images of countless nightmares. Those sights and sounds she would never be able to erase from her memory.

# CHAPTER 135

Fifty years had passed since that memorable night when the seventy-third annual Bradford Bartholomew High School prom had been held. Nadine hadn't thought about high school since she left it so many years ago or any of her classmates. As April became May, the mind suddenly seized on the name Gary Diefenbaker. She smiled as she recalled his half-hearted hallway prom proposal. She decided to play the game *whatever happened to.* Her guess was Diefenbaker was a door-greeter at Walmart or some sort of low-paying job. She giggled at his lack of prospects. When she found his Facebook page, she had to admit he looked distinguished with his gray hair, but what shocked her the most was he had become a prominent San Francisco lawyer. "Wow," was all she could say.

The mind seized on another name, Rebecca Tolliver. Nadine in her *whatever happened to* game predicted Rebecca became a recording artist. Although she couldn't stand the spoiled-rotten Rebecca, she had to admit Rebecca had a beautiful singing voice. Her Facebook page revealed a much different Rebecca than what Nadine expected. "Oh my god!" Nadine cried out when she saw photos of a plump Rebecca along with her tall, handsome husband, and six equally handsome children. There were many pictures of Rebecca singing in the church choir and thousands of posts praising not just her singing but helping lost souls find a better life through song and word. Where Nadine had considered marriage and children a waste of life, Rebecca found joy and meaning in it. Nadine begrudgingly respected Rebecca not just for her singing but as a married woman and a mother.

The mind realized the *whatever happened to* game wouldn't be complete without searching for Tommy Ward. Before she accessed his Facebook page, she closed her eyes and guessed what life held for him. She imagined after high school Tommy went to college where he became a successful football player surrounded by lots of pretty girls, one of whom he married, and after college and a great career as a professional football player, he became a brilliant forensic scientist. She smiled at her predictions, certain she was right because if anyone in her graduating class was most likely to succeed, it was he.

When she opened his Facebook page, his handsome face smiled back followed by numerous pictures of him in his football uniform with glowing newspaper and Internet articles of the *brilliant young quarterback.* She smiled that at least half of her prediction had been right. As she scrolled further down the page, she saw familiar names of classmates mourning the loss of such a great talent and a wonderful young man. Then came the page with Tommy's photo surrounded by black ribbons with the year he was born and the year he died. A short eulogy followed: *You were with us for just twenty-one years, Tommy, but you'll always live on in our hearts.*

Uncontrollable emotion overwhelmed Nadine. She sobbed bitterly. It couldn't be true. Tommy couldn't be dead. He was so perfect: smart, handsome, athletic. He just couldn't be dead. When the initial shock faded, she wanted to know how he died. She scrolled down further on the Facebook page until she found what she was looking for: brain cancer.

# CHAPTER 136

Nadine had a sudden urge to attend the fiftieth-class reunion not to see her classmates or mourn Tommy's death but to avenge it. She wanted to lash out and hurt King Tommy's followers for not having protected him from cancer's ravages. Logically she realized this was illogical, but emotionally it made perfect sense because Tommy was too perfect to die.

As May became June, Nadine made a fateful decision. She would attend the reunion not as Nadine Car but as Émile Anjou. She sent an email to Vincent Sinclair, Vice President of the Bradford Bartholomew High School seventy-third graduating class, asking permission to attend the reunion. Moments after sending it, she received Vincent's email stating she most certainly was welcome and that he was looking forward to seeing her after so many years. What he didn't tell her was few grads would attend. He attributed it to the fact no one wanted to be reminded of Tommy's untimely death. After fifty years, the pain of his passing still hadn't healed in the minds of many.

Vincent generated tremendous excitement when he emailed the graduates that Émile Anjou was going to attend. In the graduates' minds, the never forgotten mystery woman had turned a lackluster prom into an unforgettable, magical evening. Male grads frequently recounted the *intercourse* joke that never failed to bring laughter to all who heard it. Female grads still found the *intercourse* joke distasteful, but after fifty years, they were willing to forgive and forget. Nevertheless, they hoped Émile Anjou had become a fat, wrinkled old hag as some of them had.

# CHAPTER 137

When Émile entered the hotel ballroom, a huge crowd assembled to meet and greet her. Vincent heard the crowd's excited shouts of, "There she is. There she is," as Émile strode confidently across the ballroom floor. He rushed to her side. He nearly fainted when he saw her. She looked the same as she had fifty years ago: same figure, same hairstyle, same shade lipstick, and a most revealing black mini.

The assembled crowd parted as he escorted her to a throne on the raised dais. The gold-embossed placard above and behind the throne read *Queen Émile*. Next to Queen Émile's throne was another throne with a gold-embossed placard on it that read: *In loving memory of King Tommy*. Vincent turned to the crowd, held up his hand for quiet, and said quietly, "Gary Diefenbaker would like to say a few words on behalf of Tommy Ward whom we all loved and respected so very much."

Gary, dressed in an expensive silk suit, spoke eloquently about Tommy: his athletic and academic accomplishments along with several humorous stories that showed that Tommy wasn't always a perfect gentleman. As Gary struggled through a veil of tears to bring his eulogy to a close, the assembled grads joined him in tears.

Many quiet moments followed until Gary broke the silence with, "It's true we've lost Tommy, but." He paused to compose himself before he continued with, "He introduced us to a new friend, Émile." He motioned toward the standing Émile who smiled and in perfect English said, "My English is much better than it was fifty years ago. I won't need a translator tonight." It was at this point Vincent informed her that Monsieur Levesque had passed away. "No great loss," Émile said haughtily. "His French was terrible." She smiled a radiant smile that captured the hearts of those before her while the band struck up a fifty-year-old oldie. Vincent was the first to ask her to dance. After him, Gary and many others followed as she danced the night away.

The hour of midnight rapidly approached. Émile asked the band leader for a drum roll as she ascended the steps of the dais. She held up her hands for quiet. The grads turned toward her expecting a loving tribute to Tommy, to the wonderful evening she had just experienced, and to the many new friends she had made. "I have a surprise for you," she announced in an arrogant tone of voice. The grads pushed closer to the dais anxious to hear what she had to say.

Émile motioned to a man who pushed his way through the crowd and presented her with a large gym bag. Without a word, she took the gym bag and set it at her feet. She removed the expensive wig that revealed frizzy, grayish-brown streaked hair. She stuffed the wig into the gym bag from which she brought out a styling-brush to fluff out the frizzy hair into a large frizzy flower. Next, she removed the false eye lashes and placed the brown contacts in her eyes. The grads stood mesmerized not realizing what they were witnessing. Émile, rapidly becoming Nadine, removed the stylish high heeled shoes and put on a pair of badly scuffed brown flats, reached back into the gym bag, took out a shapeless garment, and slipped an ugly purple dress over the black mini. She put the high heeled shoes in the gym bag. As a final touch, she removed from the gym bag a pair of black-framed glasses and put them in place. Her transformation complete, she stood in front of an awestruck audience waiting for them to cheer her cleverness and laugh at the fifty-year-old practical joke she had played on them. Someone in the crowd yelled, "My god. It's Nadine…Nadine Car."

"Can't be," a male voice shouted back. "She's been dead fifty years."

"If that isn't Nadine Car, my name isn't Goldie Greenfield." She turned to her husband who nodded in agreement. "Herschel agrees," she blurted out.

The grads quieted as they carefully studied the person who stood before them on the dais. "My god. Goldie's right!" Olivia Petrucci Carpenter shouted. "It *is* Nadine Car."

Anger suddenly spread through the grads that she had made fools of them for fifty years. They booed and hissed: not only had they lost their beloved Tommy but now they had lost their fairy-tale princess, Émile Anjou. That was too much for them to bear.

Sensing physical danger, Nadine jumped down from the dais and moved toward the man who had given her the gym bag. He hurriedly escorted her from the ballroom to the awaiting BMW that whisked her away from where she had lived so many years ago. As the car sped into the countryside, the mind recalled the words: *you can never go home again.* "No truer words were ever written," she muttered to herself.

# CHAPTER 138

The years passed but not uneventfully. After Vetrov's assassination and China's military defeats, both nations splintered into revolutionary groups struggling for national power. With the Caliphate destroyed, the Middle East became more stable although the dark shadow of religious chaos loomed in the background. In America, Perky died of a heart attack while Jocko suffered from Alzheimer's and eventually died from the disease's slow death. Both died in prison branded traitors by those in power and unmourned by their agencies and the nation they had faithfully served.

As for Nadine, she tired of the commodity markets and became a day trader making huge sums of money in mere seconds, but in time, this type of trading became too much of a strain for a woman in her late eighties. Since she was already fabulously wealthy, she dabbled in more stable markets such as currency manipulations and various world stock markets just to keep herself amused, but her newest interest was the environment.

# CHAPTER 139

Nobody in the small village knew where the woman came from. Sarah Hogan had been the first to see her. One afternoon as she was peeking through her living room window's venetian blinds, she happened to see someone enter the old McKinney house across the street. The McKinney house had been vacant for over thirty years ever since Laura McKinney had died from tuberculosis. No one wanted to live there afraid they too would catch TB and die the wretched death Laura had.

It wasn't until the woman in question appeared in the village general store that the villagers received some information about the stranger in their midst. Villagers being villagers, they wanted to know who the woman was and what she had bought. Harley Morley, proprietor of the hardware store, reported to his neighbors that she bought gardening tools and numerous packets of vegetable seeds, that she wanted the items delivered to the McKinney house, and that her name was Mabel Evans.

Upon hearing the news, Henrietta Hudson decided to pay Mabel a visit to welcome her to the village. As a pretext for her visit, she baked one of her famous rhubarb pies as a welcoming gift. When she knocked on the door, Mabel answered. Henrietta introduced herself, welcomed Mabel to the village, and offered her the pie. She was stunned when Mabel abruptly said, "I don't eat sweets, and neither should you. Now get off my property and take that damn pie with you," whereupon she slammed the door in Henrietta's face.

When Henrietta recounted these events to the villagers, they were shocked at Mabel's incivility. Bert "Woody" Woodhead offered his two cents. "Sounds to me like she's some kind of criminal." Elvira Hoppenthaler had a similar thought. "Maybe she's in witness protection, hiding out in our village." She turned to the others. "A small village would be a perfect place for a criminal to hide." Following that line of thought, Earl Higgins had an even more spectacular speculation. "Maybe she's a murderer…in our very midst." That thought fired the villagers' imaginations along with a newborn fear of Mabel Evans.

These speculations led Farley Morley, a self-proclaimed computer expert and Harley Morley's brother, to initiate a computer search to find out who this Mabel Evans really was. After several searches, he couldn't find a single piece of information that pertained to the Mabel Evans in question. That inspired him to theorize that Mabel Evans was probably an enemy agent, for which enemy he had no idea, but he was certain she was gathering secret information about the village: information that could endanger all their lives.

The very idea that all their lives could be in danger was all Ethel Niederhausen needed to put a stop to this Evans woman before she could hurt her or one single cat in the village. Since the village was too small to have a policeman of its own, she called the county sheriff and informed him about Mabel Evans. She asked him to conduct an investigation of this unknown stranger who posed a danger not just to the tranquility of the village but to the lives of every cat and everyone who lived in it.

# CHAPTER 140

When Sheriff Hanley Martin and Deputy Peter Gonzalez knocked on the front door of the McKinney house, they were surprised when a spry old woman opened the door. "Good morning," Sheriff Martin began.

Before he could continue, the old woman snapped back, "What's good about it?"

The sheriff started to introduce himself and his deputy when she interrupted him. "Why are you here?" she asked in a venomous tone of voice.

Sheriff Martin changed his tone from friendly to demanding. "Since there is no record of you buying this house, I must ask you why you're here and proof of your identity."

"It's all legal, and that's all you need to know." The old woman closed the door. Just as the sheriff was about to knock, the door opened. "I've been expecting you since that old bitty across the street keeps spying on me."

"May we come in?"

"Got a search warrant?"

"No."

"Then stay where you are." She handed him an envelope. The sheriff looked inside where he found the deed for the house paid in full with the name Mabel Evans on it. Before he could put the deed back in the envelope, she snatched both from his hands and closed the door. Moments later the door opened. She handed him her passport. "Satisfied?" she asked sarcastically once he examined the document.

The sheriff looked her in the eyes and said, "Yes, for the moment."

"Good. Now get off my property."

# CHAPTER 141

In the months that followed, the villagers became accustomed to the craggy, eccentric Mabel Evans who dressed in long shapeless dresses, who walked everywhere in the village refusing to own a car or even ride in one, and who planted a large vegetable garden and constructed the finest compost pile not just in the village but the entire country that won her many honors from national gardening groups. Rumors of her being a murderess or spy faded away as the villagers renamed the McKinney house the Evans house and for good reason. Mabel hired villagers to repair and repaint the once dilapidated house inside and out, and she did one other thing that won the affection of the villagers. She shared the vegetables from her garden with them.

Of course, Mabel did none of these things out of the goodness of her heart. She had a plan. She intended to use the village as her base of operation to launch her environmental movement she called *Earth is Calling*. In the mornings, she worked in the garden along with several villagers whom she paid well. In the afternoons, the tireless Mabel, through Internet connections, cultivated the respect of important people in the environmental movement who became enamored with this ninety-some-year-old woman whose radical ideas they fully endorsed.

Villagers were horrified late one afternoon when five black-windowed Mercedes limousines stopped in front of the Evans house. Men dressed in expensive, black suits and women in expensive, black dresses exited the vehicles and entered the house. The villagers feared Mabel had died. It wasn't until the next morning when they saw her walking to the general store that relief spread through the village that Mabel was all right. Of course, the villagers knew better then to ask about the limousines and the people in them.

# CHAPTER 142

The following week the villagers were surprised when they received a letter informing them their village had been selected for the *Earth is Calling* three-day symposium with its featured speaker, Mabel Evans. They were honored their village had been selected and that Mabel would be the featured speaker, although they had no idea what she might speak about. What concerned them was the fact the only road through the village would be closed for days so crews could move in the necessary tents, platforms, and electrical equipment needed for the event.

As the three-day event drew closer, the villagers realized they had lost control of their lives as organizers and workers took over the village without paying attention to their concerns or property. Ida Oatway as well as the other villagers were outraged when her beautiful *flowercopia* was trampled to a pulp without so much as an "I'm sorry" from the workers. This incident along with many others angered the villagers.

As the days passed, anger in the village subsided when money flowed in at unprecedented rates.  Since no hotels existed within a twenty-mile radius, organizers and workers asked local residents if they could rent a room, and if a room wasn't available, maybe space in the attic, cellar, or even floor space wherever it might be available.  The villagers were surprised the workers were willing to pay a hundred dollars a night just to remain in the village.  They gladly opened their homes to the workers who only a few days previously had angered them.  The villagers only regret was the workers wouldn't be staying longer.

# CHAPTER 143

The day of the *Earth is Calling* symposium finally arrived. It was a picture-perfect fall day with a warm sun and a cool breeze. The village and surrounding fields were jammed with more than a million people. Huge digital screens and loudspeakers had been set up in a one-mile radius of the speaking platform so everyone could see and hear everything Mabel Evans had to say, and Mabel had lots to say.

She ascended the steps of the speaking platform not like a woman of ninety-something but as a woman in her forties, self-assured and more than ready for the task at hand. As she stood before the crowd, her thin, white hair blew in wisps at the will of the wind revealing from time-to-time the top of her sunburnt head. A shapeless purple dress hung limply about her thin body, but her frail outward appearance belied the strength within. She was on a mission to fulfill her patriotic duty: not to the nations of the world but to the Earth.

In a strong clear voice, she began. *"Earth is Calling* with pain and agony ever since humanity first trod her soils and sailed her waters for humanity has brought nothing but death and destruction to the place it calls home. Few of us throw garbage on the floors of our homes, yet day-after-day, century-after-century, that's exactly what humanity has done to its home: Earth. Humanity despoils the very resources it depends upon for its survival by over-fertilizing the soil, and once humanity has done that, it sprays tons of poisonous chemicals over the very plants and soils that ensures the development of cancer in those who eat the contaminated crops grown there. Humanity has contaminated Earth's waterways with poisonous chemicals and overfished its rivers, lakes, and seas to such an extent that it has been forced to farm fish with disastrous results both for the fish and those who eat them. The media is filled with articles of people not just getting food poisoning from eating contaminated farmed fish but dying horrible deaths from brain fever to the slow, painful destruction of vital body organs caused by parasitic worms.

"I realize those of you who have been an integral part of the environmental movement, none of what I've said is news to you. You already know these well-documented, scientific facts, but, they need to be repeated on a daily basis in every school and university in the nation so that each generation has a firm understanding what's at stake for its survival.  For without this understanding, humanity is doomed, destined to go the way of the dinosaurs, and once extinct, there is no coming back: ever. With that warning in mind, I, Mabel Evans, order not just the United States government but all governments of the world to immediately enact the following demands."

# CHAPTER 144

Mabel spoke for over three hours, but frequent outbursts of tumultuous applause added an additional two hours to her speaking time. Reporters on the scene carefully documented Mabel Evans's demands so all humanity could take heed of what needed to be done to save itself from extinction. Portia Porter, one of the reporters at the symposium, selected what she considered to be the most important points during Mabel's first day comments. The following items, in Mabel's own words, are taken from Porter's article entitled, *Mabel's Mandates.*

"We must stop the consumption of all meat products derived from animals and birds to all the fishes and shellfishes in the world's lakes, oceans, and seas. Animal and bird protein are the most dangerous protein humanity can consume, yet humanity is addicted to the very thing that is killing it. Animal, bird, and aquatic bodies contain enough fat and cholesterol in a single serving to clog arteries and cause heart attacks not just in the very old but in the young as well. One-third of individuals under forty will die from heart disease before they reach the age of fifty and another one-third after age fifty. This is medical fact. The consumption of meat has created a national medical emergency, yet the animals, birds, and the fishes have the last laugh. As humanity kills them, they kill humanity. It's their ultimate revenge.

"Humanity must stop consuming meat products, and it must shut down every restaurant, supermarket, and lunch wagon that serves artery-clogging meat products. Individuals who consume this meat poison have signed their own death certificates. Thus, it is incumbent upon humanity to heed earth's warnings and shut down these instruments of death immediately. Remember this. Meat belongs on the bodies of animals, birds and fishes: not on a bun or plate. Humanity has slaughtered mercilessly innocent animals, birds, and fishes for its eating pleasure: a selfish pursuit if there ever was one: killing for pleasure. The *Earth is Calling* for this wholesale slaughter of its precious creatures to stop and stop now.

"Humanity must look and judge itself without prejudice. For those individuals who medical science considers overweight, fat, or obese, they must be denied products that contain salt, fat, sugar, and artery clogging cholesterol. That means the overweight people of the world must consume only a plant-based diet until they reach the correct weight. Even when they've reached the correct weight, they must consume only small amounts of the four horsemen of the apocalypse: salt, fat, sugar, and cholesterol so they don't regain the weight they lost and become a drain on the public purse due to the many illnesses connected to obesity.

"Now we must consider the problem of overweight children. The single most fat-inducing product newborns consume is fatty, unhealthy milk whether it's human or animal. All babies must be fed formulas developed by medical experts that supply the necessary nutrition without the harmful effects of unnecessary, unneeded fat in a baby's diet. Remember this. Milk is for the animals from where it came and is not fit for human consumption because it was never meant for human consumption only for the survival of the animal species from which it came.

"Cities are the worst invention humanity ever invented. Cities are a waste of resources. Tons of cement and steel are needed to construct these jungles of death where rats outnumber humanity hundreds-to-one, where disease stalks the streets striking down animals and humanity alike, and because of overcrowding, humanity turns against humanity inflicting the worst injuries one can imagine on each other as crime rates soar.

"Hundreds of years ago, a few men, yes, men, because women were either forced into servitude by their husbands or stuck in smelly cities unable to improve their lot because of manmade societal restrictions. These few men were considered anti-social by so-called normal society when they abandoned cities and lived solitary lives in harmony with nature taking no more than what they needed to survive. Those men were not anti-social. They were environmental pioneers. They did what we must do. We must abandon our cities, live in harmony with nature, and use nature's resources sparingly, taking only what is needed to sustain life. That means no electricity, no use of cancer-causing fossil fuels, no pesticide leaden crops, and no killing and consuming Earth's innocent creatures. *Earth is Calling* to each of us. 'Stop the madness! Stop the pollution!' Cities, disease, crime are nature's warning to abandon our cities before Earth abandons humanity: forever.

"Animals of the land, birds of the sky, and fishes of the sea know no boundaries. They freely roam Earth's land masses and its numerous waterways. Humanity restricts its own movements with national borders and walls to protect imaginary boundaries. *Earth is Calling*: tear down these inhumane walls so humanity can have the same freedoms as animals, birds, and fishes and while humanity is at it, tear down every dam in the world so the fishes of our rivers and streams can have the same freedoms their compatriots of the sea enjoy. No walls, no dams mean a pristine, unblemished Earth and freedom for Earth's creations without the vulgarities of unnatural borders and dams.

"*Earth is Calling* to humanity that it is desecrating its once bountiful lands with overpopulations it can no longer sustain. *Earth is Calling* to humanity to decrease the number of its inhabitants or perish. We environmentalists hear the specious arguments from religious groups and radical right-wing organizations that every life is precious, that every life must be preserved no matter the cost. We environmentalists most emphatically denounce these arguments as a waste of valuable resources. Native Americans lived by the laws of nature. When individuals were no longer able to contribute to their societies, they were expected to leave their communities, take nothing with them except the clothes they wore, select a spot they considered sacred, and let nature take its course. In so-called modern civilization, we preserve life at all costs no matter if that life is one filled with unrelenting pain and agony. We must release these individuals from their miseries and return them to the elements that made them.

"What applies to the living must also apply to the non-living. Once again religious and right-wing organizations spew their venom at organizations that perform abortions. I say these ground-breaking organizations do not perform nearly enough abortions not just in this country but in every country in the world. There must be no question if a baby has any type of abnormality, it must be aborted immediately whether the parents agree to the abortion or not. This is not inhumane. This is humanity saving itself from being overrun by those who for selfish reasons would take away valuable resources from the living to prolong a meaningless life. By demanding laws that permit abortion of the deformed, we environmentalists are heeding Earth's warning that abortion must not stop with just the deformed, it must start with the unborn.

"We environmentalists know as a matter of scientific fact that the Earth can only sustain a population of one billion individuals. That is a scientific fact upon which all reputable population experts agree. Therefore, I demand all countries with a population of more than one million enact zero population programs. This means few live births for twenty-five years. During this time, only a select few in each country would be permitted to have children. These fortunate children in the years to come would populate a crime-free, disease-free, environmentally correct world: a new utopia at one with the needs of Mother Earth. *Earth is Calling* that zero population growth programs must be enacted immediately if humanity is to avoid extinction.

"Humanity must remember that Earth created itself specifically for plants, animals, birds, and fishes that existed millions of years before the recent arrival of humanity some forty thousand years ago. Humanity is the interloper. Humanity is the species that does not belong on Earth. Humanity must limit its footprint on Earth so plants, animals, birds, fishes, and yes, insects of all varieties can thrive in a utopian paradise of abundance, color, and splendor unfettered by humanity and its disregard for their very existence. Humanity will pay the price for its cruelty one day and that day is rapidly approaching if it doesn't act and act now. *Earth is Calling*: Earth is demanding that humanity enact my demands to save itself or suffer the consequences of extinction."

# CHAPTER 145

During the last two days of the *Earth is Calling* symposium, Mabel demanded the banishment of all modes of transportation: cars, trains, and planes in a race against time to reverse the devastating effects of climate change and in so doing control the rising seas that threatened the world's major cities. She further demanded the need for social equality and redistribution of wealth not just in the US but the entire world so that every individual in every nation could and would have equality with the same amount of money: $14,643 and 2 cents.

In the waning moments of the symposium, Mabel raised her hands to the sky for all those in attendance to be silent. "Whether you are here in nature's own classroom, in your homes, on the streets of your community, in a school, a factory, a ship at sea, or an airplane high above the clouds," she began, "let us all sink to our knees and place our hands on the earth, the water, and the air so Mother Earth cannot just hear but feel our plea of forgiveness."

Mabel then walked off the podium, slowly sank to her knees, and placed her hands firmly on the ground as did millions of others around the world.  "Oh, Mother Earth," she intoned, "we heartily seek your forgiveness for the reckless damage we have inflicted upon your body by tearing apart your mountains, plains, and underground recesses in search of your life-giving resources in a vain attempt to enrich ourselves, that we have torn apart the bodies of your innocent creations: the animals, birds, and fishes: for our eating pleasure.  Please forgive us as we pledge from this day forward to rectify our past recklessnesses with a new beginning based upon the equality of species and the preservation of the beautiful world you have created for us.  We hereby pledge through our deeds and actions our devotion to you, Mother Earth, forever and ever."

# CHAPTER 146

Once the symposium concluded, Mabel appeared on numerous media programs where she won the hearts, minds, and souls of millions of Americans for having the courage to state truths not only about environmental and population issues but offering important solutions to these pressing problems. All media declared Mabel Evans a national treasure. Three months later she was awarded twin Nobel Peace Prizes for her groundbreaking theories and solutions in the sciences of the living environment and population control. With these and many other awards, Mabel Evans was crowned the Mother of the Worldwide Environmental Movement. From that moment on, her adoring public called her Mother Mabel. Every environmental group in the world wanted her to speak at their symposium at a million dollars per speech. In the years that followed, Mabel flew around the world in first class luxury, stayed at the finest hotels, and only ate organically grown vegetables, fruits, and nuts.

Mabel was especially pleased when the Indian government asked her to speak at a national forum where abortion legislation was to be discussed.  For centuries, the Indian government had refused to address the over-population problem, but with poverty increasing at an alarming rate, the government realized the out-of-control birthrate was depressing India's ability to progress.  It desperately needed to justify why a zero-population program had to be implemented as soon as possible.  Mabel gladly accepted the Indian government's invitation to speak at the abortion symposium, gratified her demands were seriously being considered despite strong opposition from India's religious leaders.

The one-hundred-seven-year-old Mabel stood on a small platform behind the lectern that bristled with microphones so the millions assembled before her could hear her message as well as all of India and the world beyond.  When she concluded her comments, the audience gave her a standing ovation along with thunderous applause.  She smiled and basked in the audience's adoration when she suddenly fell face forward into the lectern, slipped off the raised platform, and collapsed onto the floor.  By the time doctors reached her, she had expired.  Later that same day, doctors determined the Mother of the Worldwide Environmental Movement, the beloved Mother Mabel, died of a massive stroke.

# CHAPTER 147

Susan Welch attended one the nation's most prestigious universities where she completed not just her undergraduate program but also her master's degree. The main reason she attended the university was she wanted to continue her Ph.D. studies with the renowned criminologist, Dr. Thaddeus Timmons, who specialized in investigating not just cold criminal cases but the backstories of various individuals to understand why they had done what they had done.

Dr. Timmons was more than pleased when he received Welch's application to enter his Ph.D. program and readily accepted her as part of his research team. He assigned her to a case that was over one-hundred-years-old. The case in question involved the FBI and an agent named Bud Perkins. The question Dr. Timmons wanted answered was: why had Perkins, an FBI agent with years of meritorious service, gone rogue?

The Perkins FBI file had been sealed for seventy-five years after his death: a time period that had more than expired. This enabled Welch free access to his files that spanned more than thirty years of FBI service. When Welch looked over the files, she was delighted Perkins had kept such detailed records of every operation he undertook which made her job that much easier.

After many months of intensive research, she came upon the Luther Wilson case. It wasn't Luther Wilson who attracted her attention but a young, frizzy-haired girl that Chicago P.D. surveillance had uncovered. Welch decided to focus on the girl because there was no reason a young, white girl should have been in a black, south-side Chicago lock-shop.

Several hours of research revealed the name of the lock-shop girl, Nadine Car. It was then the Perkins case began to come together. Perkins had linked Car to numerous robberies of the rich and famous through photo identification. It was at this point Perkins decided to go rogue. He had the perfect instrument to complete his own agenda: a woman who spoke many languages, had nerves of steel, and was attractive. He wasn't about to turn her over to a corrupt FBI that would lock her up in some prison for years until she was of no use to anyone. Perkins blackmailed Car into working for him. Her choice had been either work for him or go to prison.  Once Perkins had Car on his team, he confiscated her cell phone which led to lab techs breaking the phone's Crypto-Coin codes that led to the destruction of the virtual currency.  Welch smiled when she read Perkins had given Car the code name Chameleon because she was a master of disguises.

Perkins also enlisted the services of a top CIA agent called Jocko so named because he had been a star football player before he joined the agency.  In Perkins's and Jocko's first rogue operation, the two agents placed Car, disguised as a waitress, in a diner to spy on the Russians.  Car learned about the Russian's drug and child prostitution operations, the plan to collapse the British and American economies that led to the Russian president's assassination.  Perkins and Jocko smashed the drug and child prostitution operations and with the aid of Sir Roger Fitz-Alan, head of Britain's MI6, foiled Vetrov's plan to collapse the British and American economies.

Welch began to appreciate the deep involvement of Perkins, Car, and Jocko who had risked their lives to save the lives of millions.  Welch's admiration for Car increased exponentially when she read about Car's one-hour exploit with the leaders of the Caliphate and how she, disguised as a representative of a virtual currency syndicate, had seduced them into investing two-hundred-million dollars in a bogus crypto currency. "Wow," was all the breathless Welch could say when she finished reading the file.

Welch rated Car's service as a nanny in the Chinese embassy as the boldest bit of spying she had ever read about or seen in a movie. Numerous photographs taken by various agents while Car, disguised as a nanny walking in Central Park, revealed an unattractive, unassuming woman who attracted little female and even less male attention. The fact that Car was able to belittle the Chinese ambassador's ten-year-old boy by calling him a *dull child* on a daily basis to such an extent that the boy needed to prove his worth by disclosing Chinese military secrets was, in Welch's view, a brilliant mind-altering strategy of subtle denigration over a prolonged period of time.

Once the American and Israeli attacks against Chinese and Iranian military installations concluded, the Perkins files ended with a terse prediction that both he and Jocko expected to be arrested, incarcerated, and branded as traitors by their respective agencies. Tears came to Welch's eyes as she realized the tremendous self-sacrifices these unsung heroes of intelligence gathering had been willing to make to serve their country.

One mystery remained.  Whatever happened to Nadine Car?  Welch needed to have more information about all three individuals.  She realized she had to dig deeper into their backstories to find out what made them tick and why they did what they did.

# CHAPTER 148

Welch's research into Perkins's childhood revealed he had been born in a large city, had middle-class parents, was a below-average student, and wasn't popular in school. In fact, the other kids made fun of him because he had been severely overweight throughout his elementary, middle, and high school years. His teachers considered him a *directionless plodder* with little to no ambition. It wasn't until he was in his third year of college that a guest lecturer, an FBI agent, was invited to speak to his sociology class. The agent discussed the sociological environments that produce criminals and why many individuals can't accept a life without crime.

The lecture fired Perkins's imagination. Before the agent had finished, Perkins vowed he would become an agent. He studied hard to meet the FBI's educational requirements, put himself on a strict diet, and exercised hard to build up his body to meet the physical requirements. Once he was accepted as an FBI agent, he became a plodder but of a different kind. He focused all his energies on just one thing: the assigned case. He worked longer hours than he had to and refused to close a case until he solved it. These attributes won him citations for meritorious service along with the respect of the department and his fellow agents. As for Perkins having a love-life, Welch couldn't find a trace of one. He seemed to have had no interest in sex.

Gianni was also born in a large city. His parents were upper middle-class. His grades were above average, but his real interest was sports. He played baseball, intramural basketball and football at an early age without distinction. He was just one of the kids having fun with the other kids. It wasn't until high school that his classmates dubbed him Jocko when he became a football superstar: a name that followed him to college and later to the pros. His football fame made him a lady's man. He wasn't movie star handsome but handsome enough to attract beautiful women to his bed: one of whom he married. When he joined the CIA, his football reputation followed him, but he didn't use it to his advantage. Instead, he dedicated himself to becoming the finest agent he could distancing himself from his previous years of fame and like Perky devoted his life to his work which cost him his marriage. His childless wife of nine years divorced him on grounds of abandonment and an irretrievable breakdown in their relationship.

Welch had a more difficult problem researching Car because there wasn't much information available except she was born in a small town, had a middle-class family background, and had terrible grades in school. The only other information she could find relating to Car's schooling was a short report by a Madeline Eckhart-Cochran, a social-worker at the Percival Peabody Preparatory School, who, after a visit to the Car residence, complained that the fourth grader Car wore hideous long dresses citing in particular a long, purple dress she found particularly offensive. Then there was the follow-up phone call to Eckhart-Cochran's visit to the Car residence by the psychiatrist Dr. Sidney C. Grimes who expressed concern in his report to the Peabody board of directors that Nadine exhibited serious psychological fixations that manifested itself in her anti-social behaviors toward others which was perhaps an expression of latent if not overt homosexual tendencies or perhaps a deep inner-desire for sexual reassignment. Grimes concluded his report with the warning that the Car child must be closely monitored so she did not inflict harm on others or herself.

After several weeks of intensive research, Welch couldn't locate any additional information about Car except her senior class yearbook picture that confirmed her identity due to the frizzy hairstyle. At this point, Welch's research on Car's early years came to an end. Nevertheless, this lack of information spurred many questions in Welch's mind that demanded answers. Why was there a lack of information about Car's childhood? Did Car at an early age knowingly keep a low-profile in preparation for a life of crime, and if her grades were below average, how did she learn to speak so many languages?

Welch discussed these questions with Dr. Timmons and other members of the research team. Welch and the team built a psychological profile for Car based on the available information. The team concluded Car had been a docile child by design manipulating her parents into thinking she was an underachiever, that she was intelligent and an excellent planner able to execute her plans with impressive efficiency, that she possessed a complex psychological makeup as an introverted-egomaniac, that these contradictory personality traits would make it difficult for her to accept others as friends or have meaningful sexual experiences. This last bit of information was substantiated by Dr. Grimes's report Car had no desire to make friends which meant she was a loner, she didn't need others, and more than likely died a virgin.

The team agreed Car weaponized her beauty. Emotionally she was cold: an ice queen who delighted in hurting others. This gave her personal satisfaction as well as sexual gratification because she was able to control and manipulate others. She lived up to her code name Chameleon, changing her persona both physically and psychologically to suit the situation. The teams' conclusion: Car was a consummate thief, not a killer, that she was a person who couldn't be trusted, and that she was a bitch. This conclusion led one team member to remark, "With a friend like her, who needs an enemy."

# CHAPTER 149

When Welch concluded the Car research, she felt unsettled, as if she'd forgotten something. For reasons she didn't understand, she couldn't let go of Car. She felt there was so much more to know about her: but what?

On a wild hunch, she decided to research the videos and pictures taken at the seventy-third senior class prom of the Bradford Bartholomew's memory page hoping the frizzy-haired Car might be included in a picture or video. The grads had taken lots of selfies and videos of themselves, their dates, and someone unknown to them: a beautiful French girl. The grads wrote glowing comments, even professions of love for the mysterious young lady whose name was Émile Anjou whom they described as hot and sexy. The numerous pictures and videos they had taken from various angles revealed Émile as a young woman in the full bloom of life. Welch, however, was disappointed Car had not been in attendance.

Ever the consummate researcher, Welch remembered how Perkins had used photo identification to arrest Car for robberies of the rich and famous. She was certain Car's FBI photo ID had been erased many years ago, but just for kicks, she ran Car's yearbook photo through the FBI photo files. She was pleasantly surprised to find Car's photo ID still existed. On a whim, she decided to run the mystery French girl's photo through the FBI files. She was more than shocked when the word MATCH appeared on the screen. "Oh my god," she screamed aloud. "Nadine Car was Émile Anjou."

It took some time for Welch to compose herself and think to ask the question: *Would Car ever reveal Émile's identity to her classmates?* Welch thought about Car's profile: introverted-egomaniac, control-freak, manipulative. "Yess," she hissed to herself. *That would be in keeping with Car's personality.* Her next thought was: *Where would she reveal this revelation?* Welch pondered this question for some time before she concluded it would be in a location where the most grads from the seventy-third graduating class would be assembled. *Where would that be?* she wondered. Then she remembered what Vincent Sinclair had said at the very end of the prom. "See you all in fifty years."

"That's it," she screamed out loud.

Welch located the fiftieth-class reunion of the seventy-third graduating class in the Bradford Bartholomew High School memory book. The grads had been thrilled to see Émile Anjou especially since she could now speak English. They were as enthralled with Émile that night as they had been at the senior prom fifty years previously.

Then Émile did exactly what Nadine Car's profile predicted. Car's introverted-egomaniac personality demanded she destroy her regal creation, Émile Anjou, to prove her control over her classmates and to illustrate her superiority. She had expected cheers from the grads, praise for her cleverness at being able to execute the fifty-year-old practical joke. Videos taken before, during, and moments after her transformation from Émile to Nadine showed a confident, arrogant Nadine who stripped of the Émile disguise was shocked when the grads' cheers became jeers, and she had to flee the hotel ballroom in fear for her personal safety.

It took Welch several hours before she recovered from the shock and thrill of discovering Émile Anjou's real identity. Once she settled down, she wondered if Car had any more secrets. She carefully reread the Car files. One small detail that had eluded her for many months in the Eckhart-Cochran file suddenly made sense. Car as a fourth grader had frequently worn an ugly purple dress to school.  There was only one person, still well-known many years after her death, who had worn a purple dress.  Welch ran her picture through the FBI photo ID and once again was shocked that Mabel Evans, Émile Anjou, and Nadine Car were the same person.  Welch leaned back in her chair totally blown-away by her discoveries and uttered words she seldom used, "Holy shit!"

When Welch discussed these developments with Dr. Timmons and the research group, one important question remained in her mind.  Car had played a cruel joke on her graduating class impersonating the fictional Émile Anjou.  Had Mabel Evans done the same with her outlandish environmental and zero-population-control solutions?  Had Mother Mabel, the Mother of the World-Wide Environmental Movement, played the ultimate practical joke on not just the environmentalists but every living human-being in the world?  Welch could be certain Car had fooled her classmates, but had she fooled the populations of the world into believing what wasn't true: a lie that cost trillions of dollars and millions of lives born and unborn?  There was no way for Welch to unlock Car's last secret.  Car took that to the grave with her, not as Nadine Car but as Mabel Evans.  However, she did leave one tantalizing clue: the initials ME that suggested it had all been just about her: the chameleon.

# CHAPTER 150

Under Dr. Timmons's supervision, Welch wrote her Ph.D. thesis in which she detailed all the information she had gathered on Perkins, Gianni, and Car. The thesis was an immediate success with members of academia who read it. Welch then turned her thesis into a bestselling novel that became a smash-hit motion picture.

Once the furor over Welch's book and the motion picture calmed down, she and Dr. Timmons were determined to restore Perkins' and Gianni's good names and reputations so they would no longer be branded traitors but men who had devoted their lives and died in prison for the ideals in which they believed. Welch and Timmons lobbied Congress to honor both men *posthumously* with the highest awards for their meritorious service. Nothing passes through Congress with any speed, but after several years of persistent *nagging* as Welch liked to call it, Congress granted the demands.

Car, however, was a more difficult individual for recognition of meritorious service. Congress, especially its female members, refused to honor her *tainted service* as they so delicately phrased it. Undaunted, Welch and Dr. Timmons contacted the Bradford Bartholomew High School and requested permission to place a small plaque in the school's showcase to honor Nadine Car who, as a master thief, had partially solved a century-old crime, changed world history as a spy, and became Mother of the World-Wide Environmental Movement. Grudgingly the board of education okayed the small, unobtrusive plaque which they placed in the school's showcase.

What happened next, no one could have foreseen. Once word got out that a plaque honoring Mother Mabel had been placed in the showcase of the Bradford Bartholomew High School, the school was overrun with onlookers. The plaque was immediately removed from the school and mounted on a stone in a public park that in no time became a shrine in which thousands came daily to pay homage to the Mother of the World-Wide Environmental Movement.

The city council soon realized the park was not a suitable site for the plaque of such an infamous or famous individual depending on one's point of view. Funds were raised and within five years a museum was built in Nadine Car's honor that became one of the most visited museums in the world.  For a woman who had sought isolation and seclusion to engage in both nefarious and meritorious activities during her lifetime, in death, she became the world's most beloved historical figure never to be forgotten.

# ABOUT THE AUTHOR

Richard Paullin: he attended public schools, Mansfield, Ohio, attended Ohio State University where he earned two degrees: an undergraduate degree with a major in English and a minor in Spanish plus a master's degree in English education. He worked at various summer jobs: AMF Pinspotter, Tappan Stove, taxi driver, test tube cleaner, and chauffeur to the stars. He served in the Peace Corps, Television Educativa, Bucaramanga, Colombia. He taught English-Spanish grade levels 6-10 in four school districts: Mansfield and Wilmington, Ohio: Spring Valley and Pleasantville, New York. He retired after forty-one years of classroom service. Now he writes books to entertain readers, to share ideas with them, to inform them about events and individuals they never knew existed, and to predict the future.